# Her Patriotic Prince

## Manhattan Holiday Loves, Book 3

By

# AYLA ASHER

# Contents

# *Prologue*

♥

Laura Cunningham stood beside Carter Manheim as they observed his girlfriend, Kayla, playing with the toddler. The little boy squealed with laughter as Kayla lifted him high and swung him in a circle. The child's parents, Joy and Sam Davidson, sat on the nearby swings, smiling broadly as Kayla helped the tot expend some energy.

Laura and Carter had gone on a jog while the others played at the playground in the New York City park and they both gulped water from their containers as they watched their friends.

"It's time, Carter," Laura murmured, gaze locked on the display of revelry.

Carter swallowed, his throat bobbing. "I know," he said, staring off into the distance at Kayla.

"I can't believe how patient she's been with you. You've been dating for five years. You were clear with her about your commitment issues and she's never pushed you. Not fucking once. I'm pretty sure every other woman in Manhattan would've given you an ultimatum by now."

His lips quirked. "Yeah, she's pretty damn awesome. I never thought I'd be in a committed relationship but it's just so easy with Kayla. She gets me."

"She loves you," Laura said, glancing up at him, "and that means she'd let you wait forever to marry her. But she deserves more, Carter. It's time you man up and propose. Give her a wedding and some babies, will ya? I think she's paid her dues."

Breathing a laugh, he looked down at her. "So, basically, you're giving me the ultimatum for her?"

"Listen, buddy, I would've left your ass years ago. It's obvious you two are perfect for each other. I know you're terrified but she's thirty-eight and wants kids. And I actually think you'd be a great father, Carter."

He kicked the grass with the toe of his sneaker. "It's funny. I was always terrified of the whole 'marriage and kids' thing but when I think about having those things with Kayla," he shrugged, resting his hands on his hips, "it just seems...*normal* or something."

Laura grinned, thrilled her friend was finally going to get the full commitment she deserved. "So, you're going to propose?"

His lips curved into a sly grin. "Yeah. I bought a ring last week."

Laura punched his arm. "You could've told me that before I gave you the third degree."

Clasping his arm, he rubbed it dramatically. "Don't beat the crap out of me before I can give it to her. Geez, Laura."

Shooting him a good-natured glare, she said, "Well, hot damn. She's going to be so happy, Carter. I'm really proud of you for adulting."

"Thanks. What about you?" he asked, deep brown eyes roving over her face. "Are you ready to find someone and settle down?"

The sigh escaped, long and sad, before her lips compressed. "With whom? I'm pretty sure I've dated every guy in Manhattan at this point. I'm probably the poster child for Bumble and Match.com. I just can't seem to find someone I connect with. It's a bummer since I'd like to have a kid before my uterus shrivels up."

"Whoa," he said, holding up his hands. "When the conversation turns to shriveled lady parts, I'm out. TMI, Cunningham."

"Well, it's true. I'm going to be washed up here pretty soon."

Carter gave her a sympathetic smile. "You're hot, Laura. I say this as someone who was a self-proclaimed man-whore before I met the love of my life. You're one of the most stunning women I've ever seen and you're funny and smart as hell. Honestly, you probably intimidate the crap out of most men. Women like you don't come along every day."

"Great. I'll remember that when I'm buried under seven cats, Netflix and chilling in my lonely apartment."

"Sounds sexy," he said, winking. "Don't forget the tubs of ice cream."

Wrinkling her nose, she said, "I hate you."

Placing his arm around her shoulders, he drew her into his side. "You love me, woman. And I know you love Kayla. Thanks for being such a good friend to her. She's extremely lucky to have you. We both are."

They began strolling to the playground toward the others. "You're just saying that so I won't be mad at you."

"Obviously."

Chuckling, she placed her arm around his waist as they walked. "Thank you for loving Kayla. I'm so happy you're going to propose."

"It will happen for you too, sweetie," he said, squeezing her shoulders. "I promise. Don't say anything. I know you three can't keep your damn mouths shut.  I need to figure out how I'm going to pop the question."

"My lips are sealed," she said as they approached the monkey bars.

"Hey, guys," Kayla said, cheeks flushed as the wind flitted through her curly brown hair.  "How was the run?"

"Laura couldn't keep up with me, but I'm used to that," Carter teased.

"I ran circles around him like always," she said, scrunching her features at him.  "It was great but I'm ready for brunch and a mimosa or two."

"Let's do it," Joy said, picking up her son, George, and balancing him on her hip.  "I need a bloody Mary stat."

Together, the close-knit friend family trailed to the nearby sidewalk café to enjoy their weekly Sunday brunch.

# Chapter 1

♥

*One Year Later...*

Laura sat at the table, her teeth crunching ice from her almost empty vodka soda as she scanned the room. She'd hoped to find a hot stud to dance with at Carter and Kayla's wedding but, so far, the pickings were slim. Uncle Bob was probably the most eligible bachelor and he had a cane and smelled like Listerine. Wrinkling her nose, Laura wondered if this was what it had come to. Washed up and single at thirty-nine. Good grief, it was pathetic.

Telling herself to stop the pity party, she rose and headed onto the balcony of the sprawling banquet hall. It was one of the largest in Long Island and offered a gorgeous view of the sound. Shrouded in moonlight as the stars twinkled above, she rested her forearms on the balcony railing and stared across the dark water. There was a loneliness to the gentle liquid as it stretched before her and it comforted her somehow.

Suddenly, a tingling sparked in her spine, spreading through her body as the tiny hairs on the back of her neck stood to attention. Glancing to her left, she noticed the man approach and settle next to her, stretching his arms over the railing as well. Hmmm. He was quite presumptuous to enter her space and she found herself intrigued.

"Can I help you?" she asked, a slight annoyance in her tone.

When he tilted to face her, Laura knew she was screwed. As in, royally, head-over-heels at first sight screwed. He was gorgeous, with thick, full lips curved into a sultry smile. Ice-blue eyes pierced her under his short, dark hair. A chiseled nose and jaw completed the face of the most attractive man she'd ever seen.

"I would love nothing more than to have you help me, ma'am."

His slight Southern drawl was so sexy that Laura was sure she gushed in her thong. Telling her erratic heartbeat to chill the fuck out, she arched a brow. "Well, I'm all ears. What do you need assistance with?"

His tongue darted out to wet those full lips and her knees almost gave out. Good lord, were men really allowed to be this hot? There had to be a law against it or something, right?

"I'm just wondering why a woman as beautiful as you is standing alone on a balcony when there's a perfectly good DJ inside. Perhaps you can help me answer that question."

"I'm actually not here for the wedding with the DJ. I'm here with the one that has the live band. They're okay but I needed some air."

"Got it," he said, his eyes traveling over her bare shoulders under her silky midnight blue dress. "Who's getting married at your wedding?"

"My best friend and her super-hot actor fiancé. They're so in love it's nauseating. I only hate her a little bit." She smiled, conveying her teasing. "Who's getting married in your shindig?"

"My brother and his fiancée. Well, wife now, I guess. And same on the lovey-dovey stuff. They're deep in it."

"Yikes. Makes you wonder if they'll ever miss the days of a good ol' fashioned hook up. One and done."

Mr. Sex-on-a-Stick's eyebrow arched. "Are you into that sort of thing?"

She shrugged. "When the feeling's right. We all have needs and I like a good tussle here and there. If I feel comfortable."

He studied her for a moment. "What makes you feel comfortable...?" He trailed off, eyebrows lifted in a question.

"Laura," she said, offering her hand. He enfolded it in his, warm and calloused, and the scratch against her palm set off all sorts of sparks in her body.

"Adam," he said, shaking. "Really nice to meet you, Laura. So, you were saying, what makes you feel comfortable is..."

She gave a low chuckle. "I wasn't really saying anything of the sort, but if I was, I would say that I like to be wooed a bit and told how unfailingly gorgeous I am." She flicked her hair dramatically. "After that, I'd probably be down for some sexy times if the energy was right."

"Hmmm..." he said, squinting as he considered. "Good to know. I think I'd really enjoy making sure the energy was right with you."

Throwing her head back, she gave a hearty laugh. "Would you now?"

Blue eyes sparkled as he gazed into hers. "Oh, hell yes."

Inhaling deeply, she pondered, feeling her eyes rove over his face. "I have to go back and do a few more formal bridesmaid things but my obligations will be over in about half an hour. I have a room at the hotel next to the banquet hall so I was contemplating going for a walk on the beach before I head to bed."

"Same for me. Just a few more brotherly duties and I'm free. I'd love to escort you on your walk, Laura. Want to meet me down there by the lifeguard station in forty-five minutes?"

Laura contemplated. She hadn't had a one-night stand in a while, although she didn't mind them when the opportunity arose. She was very comfortable in her sexuality and thought sex should be enjoyed between two consenting adults if it felt right. And, oh man, did it feel right with this hunk of magnificence. Had she ever slept with anyone as viscerally sexy? Wracking her brain, she realized that was unlikely. He was a fucking Adonis.

"Okay," she said, throwing caution to the wind. After all, her best friend was married now and would be spending the night with her hot-as-hell husband. Her other best friend was married to the sweetest, most adorable man on the planet and since their son was home with the babysitter, they'd be knocking boots tonight as well. Why should she be left out of the fun? After suffering through yet another wedding as the obligatory amusing, single friend, she deserved a good time. "I'll meet you there. Don't be late."

"Sweetheart," he said, leaning in, his warm breath across her ear making her shiver, "I'd sooner lose a limb than be late to meet you on a secluded beach under the stars. See you soon." Gently trailing his fingers over her bare arm, he turned and strode away.

"Holy shit," she whispered, blood pulsing through her frame as she realized she'd just signed up for an evening with the hottest man on the planet. Determined to allow herself a night of unrestrained enjoyment, she headed back in to complete her bridesmaid duties with an almost noticeable skip in her step.

# Chapter 2

A dam Gardner trailed down the stairs from the banquet hall and removed his shoes once he'd descended the last step. Dangling them from his fingers, he waded through the thick sand, searching for Laura. She stood tall, facing the ocean, the breadth of her spine regal. Good lord, but she was beautiful. When he'd stepped out onto the balcony earlier, he'd thought she was a vision of his overtired imagination. But, no...he'd touched the silken skin of her arm and it had been so real.

Jet black, straight hair fell down her shoulders to rest atop her shoulder blades. Her dress was silky and bared much of her creamy skin to his view. He remembered her almond-shaped hazel eyes and prominent cheekbones and wanted desperately to trail his tongue over the tiny mole that sat near her upper lip. Maybe, if he was a gentleman and extremely lucky, he could make that happen.

"Hello, kitten."

She turned, her sensual lips curving into a sexy smile. "Are we at the nickname stage already?"

Lifting his finger, he traced the skin beside her eye. "Your eyes remind me of a cat's, cunning and mysterious. But if it bothers you, I won't call you that."

Her lips pursed. "I don't think it bothers me at all, actually."

"Good," he said, reaching for her hand. Her fingers threaded through his, thrilling him as she held tight. "So, how was the rest of the reception?"

"Great," she said as they began to stroll. "I'm so damn happy for Kayla and Carter. They've had a long road but it's such a happy ending."

"Did they have a lot of obstacles along the way?"

"Not really," she said, her silky hair brushing her shoulder as she shook her head. "They've always loved each other. But his dad left when he was young and it really messed him up. He was adamant about not getting married until he met Kayla. He fell for her hard. It was actually pretty sweet."

"That's nice to hear. Aaron—that's my brother—fell like that for Erika too. We're from North Carolina but he met her when he transferred to New York for work. They had the wedding here so her grandmother could come. She's too old to travel and it was really important to Erika that she attend."

"Aw, that's sweet. I hope Grandma cut it up on the dance floor."

He breathed a laugh. "Actually, she did get out there for a few. She wasn't bad."

Laura smiled up at him. "So, North Carolina, huh? I was wondering where the twang was from."

"Yep. Born and raised, although now that I've been in the navy for years it's lessened some. The more you travel, the more you lose it."

"Oh, you're a soldier," she said, waggling her eyebrows. "I should've known. Those broad shoulders must come in handy when you're on duty. I bet they look fantastic in a uniform—but the suit's not too shabby either."

"Thanks," he said, thrilled that their attraction was mutual. "I clean up pretty well. You look amazing in that dress. Is that your bridesmaid's dress?"

"Kayla let Joy and I wear whatever dress we wanted. She's pretty cool and didn't really give a damn as long as we were comfortable. We made sure our colors matched and that was it. My friends are hella awesome."

"Sounds like you're close."

"Yep," she said, nodding. "Closer than real-life sisters. They're my rocks. I can't imagine life without them."

"Do you have any flesh and blood siblings?" She stiffened a bit, causing concern to filter through his frame. "I'm sorry. I didn't mean to ask something too personal."

"It's okay." Inhaling deeply, she said, "My brother was in the army. He was killed in Afghanistan fifteen years ago. He was my only sibling."

"I'm so sorry, Laura," Adam said, squeezing her hand. "That's terrible. I've seen my share of death and injury during my experience in the military. At least he died with honor, serving our country."

"That he did," she said, chin lifting. "I'm so proud of him. His birthday was on July fourth and he always wanted to join the army. My parents used to tease him that he was an Independence Day baby through and through. When he enrolled, I think it was the best day of his life."

"A true patriot."

"For sure." Her lips formed a wistful smile. "He's buried in the Cyprus Hills Military Cemetery in Brooklyn. I go visit his grave every year on July third since it's closed on Independence Day. It's a nice tradition for me. I get to remember his birthday and thank him for making the ultimate sacrifice."

"Do your parents accompany you?"

Her eyebrows drew together. "His death was devastating for them. For all of us but really heartbreaking for them.

My dad passed away three years ago and Mom doesn't come with me.  She and I have a...kind of a difficult relationship."

"How so?" he asked, and then realized they were getting extremely personal.  "I'm sorry.  That's was an incredibly intrusive question.  You don't have to answer."

"It's fine," she said, waving her hand.  "When you've dealt with my mother as long as I have, it's just old hat."

"Wait, how long can it be?  You're, what, in your early thirties?"

She scoffed.  "Okay, your chances of getting lucky are going to diminish terribly if you keep that up."

"I'm serious," he said, gently tugging her to a stop.  Gazing at her, he didn't peg her for a day over thirty-five.

"I'm a year shy of forty, buddy.  Maybe the darkness hides my wrinkles."

"You don't have any wrinkles that I see.  Man, I never would've guessed your true age but you don't look it."

Shrugging, she began walking again, their hands gently swaying between them.  "Others have told me the same.  I guess it's good I look young since I still hold out hope of settling down one day.  It's one of the reasons my mother and I argue.  She's from a very wealthy family on the Upper East Side and is distraught that I haven't married any of the eligible douches her friends push in my path."

"Yikes," he said, chuckling.  "So, you're not a fan of old money and uptight rich dudes?"

"Nope."  Her teeth were so white as she grinned.  "Don't get me wrong, I love an expensive sushi dinner or designer dress but I've learned to afford those on a budget.  I moved out of my parents' house years ago and started a personal styling business.  My mom offered to pay all my expenses if I stayed and found a husband she approved of.  I politely declined," she said, arching her eyebrow.  "I'll inherit a trust when I turn forty but Mom wouldn't lend me any money when I informed her I was starting the business. So, I just did it on my own. I kind of left the stuffy rich world behind."

"Wow. Most people wouldn't walk away from money like that."

She lifted a sardonic brow. "It was my mom's money or my self-respect. No contest in my book."

"Well, that's really admirable. How do you like the personal styling business?"

"I love it," she said, beaming up at him. "I'm very lucky because I already had connections that I could cultivate into clients. Someone else without my family's connections would've had a much tougher time. I realize that and it almost makes me work harder if that makes any sense. I want to prove that I'm good, not because people feel obligated to hire me but because they value my service."

"It makes total sense. You're a go-getter, Laura. It's pretty fucking attractive."

Gently pulling his hand, she dragged him to a stop. Releasing her heels so they thudded to the ground, she slid her palms up his chest and encircled his neck, the scent of her hair magnificent as it invaded his nostrils.

"Adam?"

Dropping his shoes in the sand to rest beside hers, his hands trailed over the silk at her waist, gliding to rest at her lower back. "Yes, kitten." Latent desire pulsed in the low-toned words.

"Why did you ask to walk with me earlier?"

His hands tightened on her lithe frame. "Sweetheart, I don't think it takes a rocket scientist to figure that out."

Her simmering irises bore into his. "I could give you some line about how I never do this and I'm a respectable girl and all that crap, but I find I'm not really in the mood to justify what I'm about to do."

"And what is that?" he murmured.

Lifting to her bare toes, she brushed her lips against his, causing him to grow hard and turgid in his dress pants. "Why, I'm going to ravish you, of course."

He nipped her lip. "Is that so?"

"Oh, hell yes. Come here." Drawing him close, she pressed her lips against his. Adam moaned, overcome with desire as her wet tongue fought to push through his lips. Opening them, she slid in and he gasped, arms tightening around her as she plundered him. She tasted sweet and sensual, like fine champagne blended with the ripest strawberries. Craving more, his tongue searched her mouth, battling with hers, loving the high pitched mewls that escaped her throat.

Lowering his hand, he slid it over her delectable ass, cupping it through the thin fabric of her dress. Overcome with arousal, he jutted his hips into hers, holding her steady so she could feel his hard length and sense his arousal. A tremor shot through her frame and she pushed her abdomen into his straining cock, driving him wild with desire.

"You little tease," he murmured, undulating against her as he held the sweet swell of her ass in his hand. "Do you feel how hard I am? God, I want you so badly."

"I want you too," she whispered against his lips.

Resting his forehead against hers, he looked into her eyes. "You don't have to tell me anything, Laura. I sense what type of person you are. Regal and strong, like a princess who rose from the ocean."

"Wow, that's good. You've certainly got a way with words, my friend."

Smiling, he brought his hand up to cup her jaw. "I'm not looking to take advantage of you but we're both adults and we just experienced two very romantic weddings. It would be a shame to waste the idyllic sentiment of the evening, wouldn't it?"

She nodded. "It would. If you're saying all you can give me is tonight, I'm fine with that. I haven't gotten laid in quite a while. I'm okay scratching the itch."

Adam's lips twitched at her words but the cold reality of his next deployment weighed heavily on his shoulders. She must've noticed his muscles tense because she pulled back and studied him. "What's wrong?"

Drawing back a few inches, he reached for her hand, holding it as his other one stroked the skin of her upper arm. "I deploy on Monday, Laura. It's a high-level mission and I'll most likely be gone for several years. I'm not a regular officer in the navy. I'm a different type of operative. That's really all I can tell you without having to kill you." He gave her an affable wink.

"How mysterious," she said, eyes growing wide. "Is it dangerous?"

"You know better than most, with what happened to your brother, there's always an element of danger with any military operation. But I've been around a long time and am pretty good at taking care of myself."

"Wait, you grilled me about my age but I don't know yours."

His brow furrowed. "I think *grill* is a bit excessive."

Her warm chuckle surrounded him. "Okay, *discussed*. So, give it to me. Wait, let me guess. You're..." One eye squinted as she pondered. "Thirty-seven."

"Thirty-eight, but close."

"Ohhh, I'm the older woman. How exciting. I always wanted to be a cougar."

Damn, she was gorgeous and had an amazing sense of humor. How in the hell was she still single?

"I have no idea," she said, sighing, and he realized he'd accidentally blurted the question out loud. "It's not like I haven't tried. I find the men of Manhattan incredibly dull and boring. It must be me. I mean, it's the biggest city in the damn country. You'd think I'd meet at least *one* guy who does it for me."

"It's not you, believe me," he said, his tone adamant. "I've known you for about two minutes and I'm already enamored. I'm pretty sure you intimidate the hell out of most men you meet, Laura. You're incredible. It's pretty overwhelming."

Her features scrunched, making her look adorable. "Carter told me that too. I'll clutch onto those words when I'm old and single and swimming in a mound of Depends."

Throwing back his head, he busted into a deep-throated laugh. "Good lord, woman. You're too damn much." Encircling her wrists, he gently tugged her toward him, aligning the front of his body with hers. Tenderly sliding his palm over her nape, he stared into her eyes. "I wish I could give you more than one night. Honestly. I think it would be insanely fun to date you. Unfortunately, I can only give you this one. I have an early flight to DC tomorrow so I can pack before I deploy. I'm sorry it can't be more but if you let me, I'll do my best to make tonight good for you, kitten."

Laura slid her palms up his chest, encircling his neck. "How good?"

Nudging her nose with his, he almost growled. "So fucking good, baby. I promise."

"Okay," she said, brushing her lips across his. "Let's do it." Clasping his hand, she lowered to pick up her shoes and tugged him toward the hotel.  Grabbing his loafers, he clutched on for dear life and never looked back.

# Chapter 3

♥

Once they were in her hotel room, the nerves started to set in. Suddenly feeling a bit shy, which was rare for her, Laura reached up to unclasp her dress where it fastened behind her neck. Adam was there before her fingers could move. "Let me," he murmured, and she shivered, although she wasn't sure it was from the slide of his fingers against her sensitive nape or his velvet baritone. Pulling her silky hair aside, she offered him access.

Warm breath washed over her ear as he unclasped the buttons, setting them free. Turning her to face the mirror that sat atop the large brown dresser, he stared at her in the reflection. Gaze locked with hers, he slowly lowered the fabric so it fell to her waist, baring her breasts. They weren't large since she was tall and slender, but they were sensitive and her nipples pebbled in the cool air. The twin globes moved in tandem with her breathing, which was uneven and choppy.

"Look at you," he said, gliding his broad hands up her sides to cup her breasts in his palms. Touching his lips to the shell of her ear, he whispered, "You're so beautiful."

"Adam," she breathed, her nipples so tight they ached. "Please."

Sky-blue eyes bore into her as he encircled each turgid nub with his thumb and forefinger, squeezing lightly.

Lost in ecstasy, her lids drifted closed and her head fell back to rest on his shoulder. "Oh, god."

His lips trailed to her earlobe, drawing the flesh between his lips as he began to suck. "I can suck you here," he said, closing his teeth over the lobe and biting gently, "or I can suck you here." His fingers pinched her nipples again. "Your choice."

"All of the above," she moaned, her voice thick with pleasure. "Why do I have to choose?"

"Greedy little kitten," he said, biting her earlobe again. "I think I like that. It means you're going to want it all."

"Yes," she cried. "Everything you've got. If I'm going to throw caution to the wind, I'm going to take full advantage."

His tongue trailed a wet path over her ear, landing in the crevice and pushing inside. The sensation pulsed jolts of energy through her trembling frame and a rush of wetness shot to her core. Rubbing her thighs together, she realized she was almost dripping. Laura had rarely been so aroused and excitement hummed in her veins. She had no idea what she'd done to deserve such a fortuitous gift as meeting this sinfully sexy man under the moonlight, but she sent a prayer of thanks to the karma gods.

"I'll lick those pretty nipples in a minute, baby, but I'm hard as a fucking rock. I plan to be inside you multiple times tonight. Tell me what you want. I can draw this first time out or I can fuck you hard to take the edge off and then we can play. It's up to you. Either way, I win because I get to love your gorgeous body."

Laura assessed her pulsing core, quivering frame and straining nipples. A quick tussle to take the edge off actually sounded pretty damn awesome. After they were sated, they could relax and truly take the time to explore each other. Meeting his gaze in the mirror, she said, "Fuck me hard. Then we'll play."

His resulting smile was sinful. "Okay, kitten." Spreading his hand across her upper back, he gently pushed her toward the dresser. Instinctively, Laura rested her palms on the surface.

"I like to let go and talk dirty. Does that bother you? If it does, I certainly won't. I want you to feel comfortable, honey."

The corner of her lip curved. "If you hold back I'll fucking kill you."

Adam expelled a huge breath. "Goddamnit, you're perfect." Winking, he straightened behind her as she balanced on the dresser. His breath was labored as he unzipped his pants, shrugging them off along with his underwear. Reaching in the back pocket, he drew out his wallet and pulled out a condom. Ripping it open, he rolled it over his shaft.

Laura couldn't see a lot in the mirror, but her glimpse had indicated he was thick and long. Dying with anticipation, her fingers clenched the surface of the dresser. Gathering her dress in his hands, he slid it up her legs, the fabric soft on her thighs, and bared her ass to him. Hooking his fingers in her thong, he trailed it down her legs and she stepped out. Moving closer, he clutched her hip with one hand while the other aligned the head of his shaft with her slick core. Staring at her in the reflection, he rimmed her opening with the tip of his cock.

Bracing for his invasion, she pushed back into his body, causing him to growl. "Ready, baby?"

"Yes," she cried.

His hips shot forward as he inched inside her, drawing back before shoving into her tight channel again. Opening herself, she relaxed her inner muscles to allow him access. He jutted into her, slow and steady, until she asked him for more.

Leaning over her, he rested his hands flat beside hers on the surface. "You want it hard, kitten?" he asked, his warm breath in her ear so erotic. "You want my cock inside that tight little pussy?"

"Yes!" she wailed, head thrown back as her lids drew together. Struggling to breathe, she held on to the dresser for dear life.

His hands covered hers as he hammered into her and Laura thought the gesture so poignant. Although he was banging her senseless, there was an intimacy to his hands laced with hers. Feeling something shift inside her chest, she thrust her body into his, fucking him back with every ounce of energy she possessed.

"Good girl," he gritted, his voice strained from passion. "Let me make you come while you milk me." Moving his hand to her mound, his finger parted her folds. Finding her engorged nub, he began to stimulate it.

"Wetter," she pleaded, aching to come while he pounded her with his magnificent cock. After licking his fingers, he lowered them back to her clit and began circling. Laura rewarded him by bending further over the dresser, opening herself to his invasion.

He hissed a breath, taking advantage by jackknifing into her core, the walls of her tight channel enveloping him with each thrust. As his fingers circled her clit, he cupped her shoulder, holding her still while he pummeled her.

"Damn, baby," he said through clenched teeth. "Nothing's ever felt this good. I'm gonna blow my load inside that tight little body."

"Oh, god...I'm so close."

"Come," he commanded, the pressure on her clit intensifying. "I want to feel you lose it while I'm inside you."

The sound of flesh slapping together flooded her ears, so primal and erotic. Feeling as if her pounding heart might explode from her chest, she threw back her head. "Yes...coming...oh, fuck!"

Her body shattered, fracturing into a million pieces as stars burst behind her closed lids. Adam spoke words of desire to her as she came, but she didn't understand any of them. Lost in the haze of one of the most sensual moments of her life, she let herself float, feeling the walls of her center constrict around him as he groaned. Panting, she waited for him to join her and fall off the edge.

Shouting her name, he began to spasm against her. A joyful laugh escaped her throat as his muscular body rocketed into hers, his cock pulsing inside her each time he jetted his release into the condom. Collapsing over her, he heaved huge gulps of air into his lungs as he buried his face in her neck. Trembling together, he slipped an arm around her waist, drawing her into his body. It was...sweet. Protective. Primal. Laura wondered how her body fit so seamlessly against his. It was as if they were two puzzle pieces, meant to spoon against each other with perfectly cut edges. Nuzzling the short hair at his temple, she let the contentment wash over her.

"Holy shit," he murmured into her neck. "What the hell was that?"

A quick flash of anxiety rushed through her. Was he disappointed?

"Don't tense up, kitten," he said, brushing her hair from her face.  Staring into her eyes, he shook his head.  "I meant that in a good way."

Her lips curved.  "You enjoyed it?"

He pressed a soft kiss to her lips.  "I fucking loved it. Good lord.  We're going to have to do that *many* more times tonight."

Laura almost giggled.  "I'm game."

"Oh, sweetheart, I know.  It's so fucking sexy and we're just getting started."  Cementing his lips to hers, he enveloped her in a searing kiss.

Pulling back, she said in a seductive tone, "Don't threaten me with a good time."

Overcome with laughter, he slipped from her body and slapped her ass, causing her to squeal.  Then, her handsome soldier crouched down and lifted her, carrying her to the king-sized bed she'd turned down earlier.  Draping her across the sheets, he smiled down at her.  "Don't go anywhere."

He strode to the bathroom, confident in his nudity, and she bit her lip to contain her grin.  Oh, hell no.  She wasn't going anywhere.  That was an unassuageable fact.

# Chapter 4

♥

Adam munched the pizza as he smiled at Laura. Realizing that he was embroiled in one of the most amazing nights of his life, he focused on taking a mental screenshot. The next few years wouldn't be easy and he was profoundly grateful he'd found her lounging on the balcony earlier, almost as if she were waiting for him.

They'd had another round of lovemaking, slower and steadier so they could explore each other's bodies. Every inch of her skin tasted like fresh rain and he'd already memorized the feel of her tight nipples on his tongue. She was exquisite.

After round two, they'd both realized they were starving and had found a late-night pizza joint on Yelp. Laura had placed the delivery and they now lay upon the bed, lazily ingesting the pizza as they chatted. She sat against the headboard, draped in his dress shirt, only a few buttons haphazardly fastened. It offered him a magnificent view of her long legs as he stretched out below her on the bed, the pizza box between them.

"So, what's the plan with the business?" he asked, consuming the last of the crust. "Will you remain a one-person operation or do you want to scale up?"

Her lips pursed as she considered. "I wouldn't mind scaling up but I'm not sure that's what I truly want. I'm very lucky to have a huge chunk of money coming to me in less than a year and that will help considerably. By then, I hope to be married and start building a family."

Finished eating, he wiped his hands on the napkin and stared at her as his head rested on his hand, elbow pushing into the mattress. "Have you always wanted to be a mother?"

"Always," she said, wiping her hands together to brush off the pizza dough. "I want to do it with a partner but if I don't end up finding one, I'll just do it myself. My friend family is amazing and I want to raise my kids with their kids."

He cupped her silken thigh, tenderly running his hand back and forth as he spoke. "Man, I wish things were different. I'd date you so hard, kitten. You wouldn't know what hit you."

She grinned. "You'd woo me until I couldn't resist you?"

"Definitely." Moving across the bed, he grabbed the empty pizza box and threw it to the floor. Gliding over her, he loomed above, staring into her gorgeous eyes. "I'd be impossible for you to resist. And then, I'd take you home and fuck you senseless."

Her arms encircled his neck. "Show me," she whispered.

Brushing her lips with his, he licked them, slow and sensual, loving how she purred in return. Kissing a trail down her neck, he ravished the skin there before heading lower. Unclasping the buttons of his shirt, he pulled it from her and tossed it to the carpeted floor. His mouth found her nipple, a tight little beacon that called to him, and he drew it between his lips. Milking her, he reveled in the tug of her fingers as they threaded through his short hair. Wanting to push her to the edge, he lathered the stiff nub and then closed his teeth around it, biting gently.

"Fuck," she hissed, back arching to increase the contact.

"You like that," he murmured, sucking her once more to pull away the sting.

"So much," she said, her body quivering beneath him. "Again."

Murmuring in assent, he nuzzled a trail to her other breast, showering it with the same attention. Each time he tugged with his teeth she moaned; each time he lapped away the sting she purred. Already so in tune with her body, a swell of sorrow swept over him that they'd only ever have one night together. Whereas life had been fortuitous in putting her in his path, he was leaving for several years and she would most likely be with someone else when he returned. A mother to someone else's child. For some reason, it burned.

Pushing away the sentiment, Adam reminded himself to enjoy what time he had with the stunning woman who was so responsive and open in his arms. Once he'd brought her nipples to turgid, straining points, his lips blazed a path down her abdomen, his dick twitching each time her muscles spasmed underneath his tongue. Reaching her navel, he dipped his tongue inside and she clenched his shoulders with her legs. Tasting the sweet skin of her mound, he nibbled past the strip of dark hair and nudged her wet folds.

Staring up at her from between her legs, he parted her, baring her swollen core to his searching tongue. Gaze locked with hers, he licked her, long and languid, as she panted down at him. Hazel eyes shimmered behind shuttered lids; her body open as if she'd surrendered to their simmering passion as much as he. Focused on those deep eyes, the tip of his tongue began to stimulate her clit, circling with deft strokes. Each whimper from her rosy lips made him ache to bury himself inside her warmth, but he'd promised her magic and he was determined to please her.

Bringing his fingers to her nub, he circled her with firm pressure as he lowered his mouth and slipped his tongue inside her wet channel. Back and forth, he impaled her as his fingers drove her to the point of no return. With a loud groan, her body bowed, hips arching into his face as she exploded in a vibrant orgasm. Consumed with her, he buried his face in her deepest place, the shudders so sexy that his own body trembled in return. Moments later, when her body relaxed on the bed and her breath evened slightly, he rested his cheek on her thigh and gazed upon her face. Flushed cheeks...swollen lips...dazed, glowing eyes. She was the most exquisite woman he'd ever seen.

"I just..." she shook her head, the movement filled with exhaustion. "I can't do words right now."

Chuckling, he ran his hand over her hip in a reverent caress as he lay entwined with her body. "That's okay, kitten. I wanted to make you feel good."

"What about you? I can return the favor." Although he appreciated the sentiment, her eyes were drooping.

"Maybe we should take a cat nap and go another round in a few hours. Unless you want me to leave. I've never understood the rules for one-night stands. I think I'm more of a commitment guy."

Multi-colored irises studied him as her fingers sifted through his hair. "I want you to stay as long as you possibly can and only leave me when you absolutely have to. That probably sounds desperate and needy and whatever the hell else you want to call it but I don't care. You'll be gone tomorrow and I can beat myself up then."

Willing energy into his muscles, he shifted and crawled over her, drawing her into his body. Reaching for her phone, she set the alarm. "I set it for four a.m.  That will let us sleep for two hours and then I can rock your world one more time before you have to leave.  Deal?"

His grin was so wide, it must've covered his entire face. "Deal."

Reaching up, she clicked off the lamp and the room was plunged into darkness.  She draped across him, her thigh covering his, head nestled on his pec.  He stroked her hair as her fingers toyed with his chest hair.

"Hope you don't mind if I cuddle with you like a teddy bear.  I haven't cuddled in so long."

"It's heaven, kitten," he said, kissing her silky hair.  "I'd hold you like this forever if I could."

"I wish you could," she mumbled, the words garbled as her lips pushed into his chest.  "I'd like to date you too."

"I'll be back one day," he murmured, fingers flitting through her hair.  "Don't forget about me."

"No way," she whispered.

Giving into exhaustion, their breathing slowed and they fell into slumber.

# Chapter 5

Laura awoke to the sound of soft snores against her temple. It had been so long since she'd fallen asleep with someone and her arm tightened across his chest. Adam felt so solid beneath her, reminding her of her desire to find a good man and build a life with him. Now that Kayla and Joy were married, she wanted it even more. Extremely happy for her two best friends, she very much wanted to find the same.

If only Adam didn't have to trek halfway across the world for years. What a cruel twist of fate. If they had time to date and cultivate their relationship, would he be someone she could settle down with? Someone who got her sarcastic sense of humor and straightforward personality? She didn't consider herself an easy person but she knew she was fun and loyal, and when she loved someone, it was with her whole heart.

Lifting her head to gaze at Adam, she trailed a finger over his cheek, worried for him. He'd said his assignment might be dangerous. Curiosity coursed through her as she contemplated his mission.

Inhaling a deep breath through his slightly parted lips, his lids slowly opened. Sky-blue irises gazed into hers, the swirling colors within mesmerizing. "Hey, kitten. Did you have a good nap?"

Nodding, she cupped his jaw, attempting to memorize his angular features and every curve of his handsome face.

"What's wrong?"

"I was just wondering where you're going. You said it might be dangerous and I'm worried for you."

His lips curved as he sifted his fingers through the hair at her temple. "It's in Central Asia. That's about all I can say. I expect to be there for three or four years at least. While I'm away, I'm not allowed to have contact with anyone at home."

"Even your family?"

"Even my family. It's a tough gig but it's what I signed up for. Hopefully, this will be my last mission abroad though. Operatives of my kind begin to age out around forty and usually settle into domestic work like private security or join the Reserve Corps. It will be nice to have a domestic assignment once I'm done with this one."

Running the pad of her thumb over his lips, she felt her heart constrict. "Please be safe."

"I will, sweetheart," he said, strumming her soft tresses. "It's really sweet for you to worry about me."

For some insane reason, she felt the sting of tears. "I am worried. You're pretty damn awesome. I don't want you to die."

He breathed a laugh. "Me either, believe me."

"Sorry to just lay it out there," she said, wrinkling her nose. "Kayla and Joy tell me I lack a filter ninety percent of the time."

"And the other ten percent?"

She shrugged. "I'm probably eating or my mouth is otherwise incapacitated."

His deep laughter surrounded them. "Noted. I like your directiveness. There's something so sexy about a woman who speaks her mind."

"Well, you get that in spades with me, buddy."

Gazing up at her, he shook his head on the pillow. "I'm so sorry I have to deploy. What a waste to meet someone as amazing as you and have to leave the next day."

"I'm sorry too," she whispered. "Should we exchange numbers?"

His expression turned wistful. "I would but I can't contact you. It's actually for your protection. I don't keep contact information stored in my phone on the off chance I get abducted. It can lead to ransom requests and other extremely dangerous situations for the people I love. As much as it sucks, it's best we don't exchange information."

Disappointment coursed through her and she nodded.

"It's not because I don't want to, Laura," he said, palming her cheek. "If things were different...well, there are so many possibilities. But they're not and I don't want you to hold onto something I can't give you. I want you to remember this fondly and find a man who can give you everything you want. Lucky bastard. Whoever he is will win the fucking jackpot with you."

"Says the man who's running away in an hour."

"But I'm here now," he murmured, drawing her close and placing a soft kiss on her lips. "Let's shower together."

Nodding, she eased from the bed, extending her hand and tugging him behind her. Once in the bathroom, they shared her toothbrush, smiling at each other in the reflection at the intimate gesture. Adam led her into the tub, turning on the shower and drawing her close. The spray sluiced over her body as they kissed, passionate and thorough, tiny groans of pleasure escaping their lungs.

Adam stepped out to grab a condom, and once sheathed, gently urged her back against the damp shower wall. Sliding his hand behind her knee, he lifted her leg, draping it around his waist. Her heel dug into his ass, the muscles so firm, as he slid the tip of his cock between her plushy folds.

"Look at me, Laura," he commanded, gruff and urgent.

She locked onto his eyes, fearing she might drown in them.

"Whose pussy is this?'

"Yours," she cried, anticipating his invasion.

"Fuck, yes," he said, inching into her. "You're mine."

"I'm yours," she said, her lips crashing into his, drawing him into a violent kiss. "God, Adam, it feels so good."

"I know, baby," he said, his strong hips impaling her, thrusting her back against the tiles each time he fucked her. "Your body was made for me. Take me deep, kitten."

Laura slid her leg further up his back, opening wide, allowing him to shove so deeply inside she thought she might collapse in a heap of nerves. The head of his cock pummeled her, the base gyrating against her clit each time he pumped. Overwhelmed by the stimulation, she felt her control wavering.

"I've got you," he grunted, strong arms holding her until she felt weightless. "Let go, kitten. I'm here."

Her body splintered, each cell bursting open as the orgasm slammed into her. Adam groaned her name as his balls slapped against her ass, the sound of wet flesh so intoxicating she could barely breathe. Pounding her for dear life, his muscles tensed and he bit her neck, groaning so wildly that a laugh escaped her throat. They were encompassed in each other, lost to pleasure, and it felt magnificent.

Strong hips surged into hers as he spurted every drop of his release into her body. Shuddering, he murmured unintelligible words into her nape as he fell back to Earth.

Panting, she clutched him, holding on as if she'd never let go.

Heaving a ragged sigh, he began to pull out of her. Opening her eyes, she saw his expression turn to one of grave concern.

"Adam?"

"Fuck," he said, reaching for his shaft. "The condom broke. Goddammit." He lowered her to her feet and pulled off the ripped covering. "Shit, Laura. I'm sorry."

Fear slammed through her as she realized the significance of the moment. "Fuck," she breathed.

Ice-blue eyes swam with concern. "Are you on birth control?"

"No," she said, shaking her head as the room began to spin. "The pills mess up my hormones and I had a terrible reaction to an IUD, so I just don't use anything. I've always used condoms when I have sex."

"Let me clean this up and we'll figure out what to do." Stepping out of the shower, he disposed of the condom and said, "I'll give you some privacy. Come on outside when you're ready."

Swallowing thickly, she nodded as he closed the door behind him. Stepping from the tub, she sat on the toilet and relieved her bladder. Wiping the evidence of their loving, she noticed his milky release on the tissue paper. Son of a bitch, it was *everywhere*. Anxiety pulsed through her still sated frame as she cleaned up and wrapped a towel around her naked body. Striding into the room, she observed him as he sat on the bed. He'd donned his boxer briefs and wore a somber expression.

"It's okay," she said, although she wasn't sure if she was assuring him or herself. Approaching him, she sat beside him on the soft mattress. "I can stop at the pharmacy and get a morning-after pill. It's not a big deal."

He took her hand, lacing their fingers. "I'm clean, Laura. It's important to me you know that. I have to get tested regularly and, honestly, I don't hook up all that much. I don't want you to feel unsafe with me."

"I'm clean too," she said, squeezing his hand. "I just got tested six months ago and, sadly, haven't gotten any action since then. Until you came along." She gave him a tender smile.

His nostrils flared as he inhaled and lifted a hand to brush the wayward tendrils at her forehead. "As far as pregnancy goes, if you're okay getting the morning-after pill, that seems like a good solution. I'm so sorry, sweetheart. This sucks."

"It's not your fault," she said, facing him and draping her arms across his shoulders. "Shit happens. I wouldn't trade anything for the night we just shared, Adam. It was so special to me."

"To me too, baby," he said, placing a sweet kiss on her lips. "You're remarkable. I'm going to think of you so often while I'm away."

She snickered. "It sounds like you're going to jail."

"Without you, I might as well be."

The words were so poignant, said as he gently brushed her hair from her temple. If their situation was different, she could see herself falling in love with this man. He was everything she'd ever searched for and never found.

They stared at each other for a few reverent moments and then he rose to dress. Laura lay back on the bed, discarding the towel and pulling the covers over her flushed skin. Once dressed, he sat on the bed and picked up the pen that sat on the bedside table. After jotting something on the notepad, he released the pen and smiled. "Just in case. Only use that for emergencies, okay?" Lowering, he rested his palm beside her head and stared into her eyes. "If you're pregnant and you need me, please call me, Laura. I'm not the kind of guy who leaves a kid behind. I'd want to help you in any way I can."

Laura nodded, hating that he had to leave. "Okay," she whispered.

"Promise me."

Cupping his cheek, she ran her thumb over his lips. "I promise."

He touched his lips to hers one last time, a wistful yearning in the gentle movement of his mouth against hers. Laura's tongue swept out and washed over his, memorizing his taste. Drawing back, he caressed her cheek. "Goodbye, my sweet, sexy kitten. You were the best damn thing that could've happened to me this weekend. Thank you."

"Thank you," she said, unable to control the tear that trailed from her eye to her hairline.

"Don't cry, sweetheart," he warbled, his voice thick with emotion.

"Please don't get hurt. I'll be thinking of you. Probably more than I should."

His smile was sad but undeniably sexy. "So will I. I'm pretty sure your face is ingrained in my brain, and that's pretty damn awesome since you're so fucking gorgeous. Bye, Laura." With one more gentle peck, he rose from the bed and strolled to the door. Giving her an affable salute, he exited the room, the door clicking softly behind him.

Laura exhaled a huge breath, the significance of the evening too much for her to process as emotion swirled through her frame. Sadness that he was gone. Fear that the condom had broken. Elation that she'd made love to the sexiest man she'd ever met. Unable to manage the maddening emotions, she closed her eyes and fell into a restless slumber.

# Chapter 6

♥

Hours later, Laura jolted awake. Harshly rubbing her eyes, she uttered a mild curse. Searching for her phone on the bedside table, she unlocked the screen, observing the time. Eight twenty-seven a.m. Joy and Sam were going to give her a ride back to Manhattan in their rental car at ten. That would give her plenty of time to grab some coffee and research how to get her hands on a morning-after pill.

Throwing on jeans, a tank top, and sandals, she headed to the lobby to grab a cup of complimentary coffee. As she squished it from the large metal container, it smelled fantastic. It probably wasn't gourmet, but she wasn't a morning person and absolutely could *not* function as a human each day without her standard two cups of coffee. Trailing back to the room, she sat on the edge of the bed and looked at Adam's jotted note.

*Adam Gardner, 202-385-6634*

Gazing at the ceiling as she contemplated, she decided that Gardner was a fine last name. Simple and functional. *Laura Gardner.* It had a nice ring. Rolling her eyes, she mentally scolded herself for traveling to temporary la-la land. Picking up her phone, she searched for info on the morning-after pill.  Luckily, in New York City, a person could purchase it over the counter from any pharmacy.  Deciding she'd stop by her local pharmacy once she was home, she reached for her coffee.

Taking a sip, she cursed, the hot liquid burning her tongue. Taking the top off, she blew on it, hoping to cool it down. Suddenly, a loud knock sounded on her door and she jolted, the coffee flying from her hand.  It landed on the bedside table, drenching the pad where Adam had written his number.

"No!" she screamed, jumping into action to save the information.  Lifting the pad, she shook droplets from the paper, trying to save the lightly-written digits.  Reaching for one of the napkins from their late-night pizza fest, she blotted the pad dry.  It was no use.  The paper was soaked through and the numbers were illegible.  They bled into the page, stained with black coffee, unreadable and destroyed.

"Goddammit!" she screamed, furious at whoever had knocked on her door so abruptly.  Stomping toward it, she yanked it open.  "What the hell—?"

The dazed look on Sam's face stopped her cold.  "What's wrong?" she asked.

"Carter and Kayla were in a car accident on the way to the airport for their honeymoon.  She's not seriously hurt but he's in critical condition."

"What?" she breathed, covering her heart with her hand. Stepping back, she fell onto the corner of the bed.

"I know," Sam said, sitting beside her and pulling her into a firm embrace.  "Joy's a mess.  She made me come and tell you because she can't stop crying.  They're at LIJ Hospital and we're going to head straight there.  I figured you'd want to come with us."

"Damn right I do," she said, lifting her chin. "Let me pack. I'll be ready in five minutes."

"Okay. We're in room one forty-nine. See you soon."

Placing a loving kiss on her head, he stood and stalked from the room. Running her hands through her hair, Laura raced into action. Carter was hurt and she was desperate to be by his side and comfort Kayla. Thoughts of the morning-after pill flew out of her frazzled brain as she packed. It could wait. This was much more important. Zipping her bag, she jogged down the stairs to meet Sam and Joy.

S itting in the staid waiting room, Joy absently bit her thumbnail as Laura sat beside her, lost to her own thoughts. Sam had gone to get them coffee and they waited for Kayla to return from the ICU to give them an update. Gazing up, Laura saw her walk around the corner. A bandage covered her forehead and her arm was in a sling, showcasing how close she'd come to being more critically injured as well.

Laura and Joy both leaped from their seats, rushing to her side and dragging her to sit between them. Burying her face in her hands, they let her cry as they soothed her, gently rubbing her shoulders and back.

"We're here, sweetie," Joy said in her always-sweet tone. "It's going to be okay."

"What if it's not?" Kayla asked, the words wrenched from her throat as she glanced between them with her tear-streaked face. "How could this happen? How could I go from experiencing the happiest day of my life yesterday to the absolute worst possible scenario today? It's so fucking unfair."

"It is unfair," Laura said, tucking a brown curl behind her ear. "Life blows sometimes, sweetie. But you've got us and we're not leaving your side until Carter is awake and healthy and driving us all nuts like he loves to do. I mean it."

"Thank god you two are here. I love you so much." Kayla's chin warbled as she grasped Laura's hand. "I couldn't get through this without you."

"I know," Laura said, determined to stay strong and stoic for her friend. "We've got you, K. Cry all you want to. I'll grab a damn bucket to collect the tears if I need to."

Kayla breathed a laugh. "That's very poetic, Laura."

"There's more where that came from," she said, settling into the chair and draping her arm over Kayla's shoulders. "I'll wax poetic for you all damn night. Might as well put my stupid historical literature college minor to use. Where to start? Ah, the virtues of D'Artagnan and the Three Musketeers. My favorite character was Milady de Winter..." She trailed off, drawing them into the meaningless dribble so their minds would drift from the severity of Carter's injuries. They stayed there long into the day until the sun slid behind the horizon and moonlight filtered through the hospital windows.

Laura stirred around three a.m., her neck popping as she stretched in the uncomfortable chair. Kayla had urged them to leave and she and Joy had promptly told her to stuff it. No way in hell would they leave her when she needed them by her side. Standing, she placed her hands on her lower back and stretched, and then headed to the bathroom on the waiting room floor. Kayla, Joy, and Sam were all sleeping in the crunched chairs as well and Laura realized they'd need some serious yoga once Carter recovered.

Taking care of business, she sent a prayer to the universe, hoping Carter would be okay. Man, if he didn't start to recover soon things were going to go downhill. Kayla was already hanging on by a thread and they all were frazzled. Washing her face and hands, she noticed the bags under her eyes in the mirror. It made sense since she'd spent most of the previous evening knocking boots with only a few hours of sleep, and the rest of the weekend at the hospital. Craving the softness of her own bed, she yawned.

Reaching in her bag, she pulled out the now-dry notepad. Only Adam's first name was legible. The rest was faded into nothingness. Running her finger over the parchment, she realized how much she missed him. Strange, since they'd only spent a few hours together, but she'd felt a connection with him all the same. Sending another prayer to the heavens for his safe passage to Central Asia, she returned to the waiting room.

Around ten a.m. the friend group finally got the news they'd been hoping for. The doctor informed Kayla that Carter was breathing on his own and the breathing tube had been removed. She promptly scampered to his room, leaving Laura, Joy, and Sam behind. When she returned, she was beaming through her tears.

"He's going to be fine, guys," she said, collapsing on a chair and hugging her waist. "Oh, my god. He's going to need a lot of physical therapy but he's going to be fine. I'm so relieved."

Joy and Laura held her, so thankful for his positive prognosis, and eventually left the hospital early that afternoon. Once Laura was home, she took a shower and flopped into bed, telling herself she'd sleep for a few hours and head to the pharmacy before it closed. When she opened her eyes, a stream of early-morning sunlight filtered through the window.

"Shit!" she said, jackknifing to a sitting position and checking her phone. It was six-thirty a.m. Googling local pharmacies, she saw that the closest one didn't open until eight. Frustrated she'd slept through the night, she now realized the effectiveness of the pill would be extremely minimized.

Still, she trudged out of her apartment at seven forty-five and was at the pharmacy as soon as the doors were unlocked. Walking under the fluorescent lighting, she spoke to the pharmacy tech, explaining that she needed the Plan B pill.

"Did you have intercourse last night?" the female pharmacist asked, walking over.

"No," Laura said, rubbing her forehead with her fingers. "It was over forty-eight hours ago."

The pharmacist nodded, and Laura was thankful for her professional tone. There was no judgment in her words, just a calm regurgitation of information. "We can sell you the pill but the effectiveness will be severely diminished with the time that has passed. As long as you understand that, Samina here will ring you up."

"I understand," Laura said, pulling out her wallet. The transaction seemed cold somehow as Samina ran the plastic through the processor. Clutching the waxy paper bag, she walked home, her mind reeling.

Once she was in her bathroom, Laura stared at her reflection in the mirror, contemplating. A thirty-nine-year-old woman stared back at her. One who had always wanted children and was ready for that step in her life. One who felt a deep connection to the man she'd lain with in passion and intimacy, although they barely knew each other. It made no sense, but she felt it all the same.

Pulling the Plan B box from the bag, she considered it. Then, she placed it in her cabinet drawer and closed it tight. Cementing her decision, she stared into her own eyes. If she was lucky enough to have a baby from the brief encounter with Adam, she would love the child with all her heart. Firm in her decision, she gave herself a nod and prepared to meet her client later that morning.

# Chapter 7

♥

***Six Weeks Later...***

Carter ambled along on his cane, frustrated his leg wouldn't open to a wider stance.

"Come on, grandpa," Laura said, arm around his waist as he huffed. "How am I going to run circles around you again if you can't even walk? Pick up the pace!"

"Damn, Laura, you're a real Nurse Ratchet. Chill. I'm trying."

"There's no try, only do. Did Yoda teach you nothing?"

Suddenly, he groaned and halted. Concern flooded Laura. "Carter? Are you okay? Where does it hurt?"

"Here," he said, tapping his cheek with his finger. "I need you to give me a big smacker."

Realizing she'd been played, she punched his arm. "Asshole! I thought you were really hurt. Damn it, Carter. You gave me a heart attack!"

"I'm fine, Cunningham. I just need some space, geez. When you told Kayla you'd walk with me to replace our runs, I didn't realize you were a damn drill sergeant."

She crossed her arms, tapping her foot as she shot him a scolding glare. "Kayla and I both love you and want you to get better. So, it's my way or the highway, buddy."

"Man, you're tough.  Okay, let's do it.  Only a few more yards to the picnic area.  I think I can make it."

Sliding her arm across his back, she helped him amble to the spot where Kayla, Joy, Sam, and George were sitting at a picnic table.  "Hey, guys," Laura said.  "I only wanted to kill him seventeen times today.  We're making progress."

Kayla stood and lifted to her toes to kiss her husband.  Then, she enveloped Laura in a huge bear hug.  "I love you so much," she whispered in her ear.  "Thank you for walking with him.  He enjoys it and it's helping him get better."

"Of course, K," she said, squeezing.  "I'm just so glad he's okay."

They sat at the table, Laura grabbing a handful of Doritos and munching on them as she eyed her friends.  Joy wore a shit-eating grin and Laura's eyes narrowed.  "What's up, J? Your face is weird."

Joy's features scrunched.  "Well, that's rude."

Laughing, Laura wiped her hands together, divesting them of the powdery cheese.  "Sorry.  You're just doing a...thing," she said, circling her hand over her face.  "What's going on?"

"Well, it probably has something to do with the news I just told her," Kayla said, beaming.  "I'm eleven weeks pregnant, Laura.  We're going to have babies!"  She clutched Carter's hand as he stared at her with love.

"Babies?"

"We're having twins," Kayla said, beaming.  "Apparently, they run on Carter's dad's side of the family."

"My swimmers are awesome," Carter said, shrugging. "What can I say?"

"No way!" Laura squealed, rushing over to hug her. They swayed back and forth for several seconds and pure happiness jolted through Laura.  Kayla had wanted kids for a while and she was thrilled they were embarking on the next step in their journey.

"It's unbelievable," Kayla said, drawing back. "I'm so excited, Laura."

"Eleven weeks, huh? Guess that shoots down the notion you two had a virgin wedding."

Kayla's cheeks flushed, making her look extremely pretty. "We started trying a few months before the wedding. Figured it was pointless to wait."

"And trying is really fun," Carter said, waggling his eyebrows.

Laura laughed. "See? I told you it was worth it to make a commitment to her. Nice job, Carter. Glad your stud muffin sex practices are paying off."

"You know it," he said, huffing on his fingernails and rubbing them on his shirt, appearing extremely satisfied.

"Oh," Kayla said, turning and picking up a container from the table. "I can't have sushi anymore because I'm preggers and Joy and Sam were thoughtful enough to bring me this spicy tuna roll from Trader Joe's. Do you want it? I know you love spicy tuna too." Kayla lifted the tray toward Laura and the smell of raw fish permeated her nostrils.

Nausea swept over her and she gulped a huge breath. Then, she doubled over and proceeded to puke all over the lush green grass.

Upon finishing the most epic barf session of her life, Laura straightened and wiped her mouth with the back of her arm. Grasping the napkins that Kayla thrust at her, she ran them over her lips, feeling disgusting. Closing her eyes, she inhaled several deep breaths.

"Holy crap, Laura," Kayla said, rubbing her back. "Are you okay?"

Joy had rushed to her side while she was expelling the contents of her stomach, and she ran her hand over her hair. "Laura? Was it something you ate? Do we need to take you to a doctor?"

"No," Laura said, waving them off. She loved them dearly but their attention was stifling. Stepping back a few paces, she held up her hands. "I'm fine guys. My stomach's just messed up."

"You just puked like a sailor at sea for forty days. I think we should take you to the doctor—"

"I'm pregnant," Laura interrupted, squeezing her eyes closed. This certainly wasn't the way she'd wanted to tell them but her tolerance for patience was running thin. "About six weeks. So, yeah, there's probably going to be a lot of puking for me over the next few months. Maybe K and I can have a contest." Lifting her lids, she contemplated her friends.

Kayla stared back at her, stunned, mouth open as the wheels churned in her highly intelligent brain. Laura could almost see her calculating as she did the math to determine when Laura had conceived. Joy wore an expression of surprise laced with a slight hurt that shifted something in Laura's heart. She'd never meant to keep her one-night stand or the possibility of her pregnancy from them. It had just...happened. Life had been consumed with Carter's recovery and there just hadn't been a good time to discuss it.

"You're pregnant?" Joy asked, crestfallen at Laura's concealment.

Sighing, Laura rested her hands on her hips. "I'm sorry, guys. This isn't how I wanted to tell you. Damn it. It's a really long fucking story."

"Earmuffs," Sam said, covering George's ears with his hands. "I think us fellas should let you three talk. What do you say, Carter? The game's on and I've got beer in the fridge."

"Yes, please," Carter said, standing. "I get the sense it's about to go down. Maybe move tables, ladies. Laura pretty much ruined the grass by this one."

Shooting him a scowl, she stuck her tongue out at his resulting wink. They gathered the food in the picnic baskets and trailed home with George in tow as the three friends silently stood, assessing each other.

"I'm down with Carter's idea. Let's find a new table or I'm going to be sick again. Come on and I'll tell you guys everything." Laura led them to a vacant picnic table several feet away and they sat across from her, gazes wary.

Spreading her palms on the cement table, she struggled with what to say. "I didn't know how or when to tell you guys. With everything that happened with Carter, my own problems just kind of fell to the wayside."

"That's bullshit, Laura," Kayla said, anger in her brown eyes. "We're your best friends and you're supposed to tell us everything. How could you think we wouldn't be here for you?"

Running a hand through her hair, she contemplated. "I met Adam the night of your wedding. His brother's wedding was the one next door. He was insanely hot and chivalrous and we knocked boots. I was all set to tell you guys until Sam showed up at my door and told me about your accident. Then, I just didn't give a damn about anything else."

"Oh, Laura," Joy said, reaching over to grab her hand. "You met a nice, handsome man. That's wonderful. I want to meet him."

"Um, yeah, that's impossible since he's halfway across the world and untraceable."

"What?" they both said in unison.

Laura updated them on Adam's deployment, her unfortunate incident with the notepad and spilled coffee, and her ultimate decision not to take the morning-after pill.

"Wait, like, you can't read his number at all?" Kayla said. "Are you sure?"

"Here," Laura said, pulling the pad from her purse. "Give it a try. I carry that damn notepad everywhere. I feel like one day I'm going to be able to decipher it. So far, no such luck."

Kayla studied the parchment, lifting it high in the air and squinting. Joy did the same before setting it on the table and shrugging. "I can't decipher the number, only his first name and a 'G' after it."

"Gardner," Laura said, smiling wistfully. "That was his last name. Simple and sweet."

"Wow," Kayla said, eyes wide. "You really liked him."

Laura nodded. "I really liked him."

"And now you're carrying his baby."

Laura blew a breath over her extended bottom lip, fluttering the hair at her forehead. "Yep. I'm an unmarried pregnant hussy from a one-night stand. Can't wait to tell my mother. She's going to flip her shit."

"Let's put her in a room with my mom and ply them with alcohol," Kayla said. "They're both drama queens and can drown in their disappointment of us together while we create fabulous lives for ourselves."

The corner of Laura's lips curved. "Sounds perfect."

They joined hands, completing the circle that had always comprised the three of them. Laura had never been closer to anyone in her life than these two amazing women.

Threading her fingers through theirs, she smiled. "I'm strong, guys. I wanted this pregnancy. I knew what I was doing when I didn't take the morning-after pill. I'm going to have this baby and raise her with your babies and they're going to be awesome humans who are going to do great things in this world."

"You think it's a girl?" Joy asked.

"Yeah, I just feel it or something. I mean, if it's a boy I'll be thrilled too. Either way, I'm pretty damn happy about it, guys."

"You're so damn amazing, Laura," Kayla said. "I'm with you every step of the way. You have no idea how excited I am that we're going to experience this together. We can go to Lamaze together and read baby books and nest. Oh, man. It's going to be so fun."

"And I'm here for anything you both need," Joy said. "Since I'm a pro at this already." She snickered and gave a self-deprecating eye roll as they devolved into laughter. There, under the bright midday sun, Laura was overwhelmed by how lucky she was. The next chapter of her life was upon her and she was ready to face it head-on.

# *Chapter 8*



***Four Years Later...***

"What dress do you want to wear today, baby?" Laura asked her daughter as she perused the closet. "Red or blue."

"Blue," Chloe said. "The one with the butterflies."

"Butterflies it is." Grabbing the cute frock, Laura crouched down and slid it over her head. Dark hair stood straight from static electricity as Laura tugged the dress in place. Then, she slid her fingers through Chloe's hair, dampening the static so it sat silky and smooth on her shoulders.

"You have your Mama's hair, baby," she said, touching her finger to Chloe's nose. Her tiny features scrunched, sending a jolt of love through Laura's heart. She was the most adorable human she'd ever beheld and the love she felt for her was purer than any she ever could've imagined.

Chloe ran her fingers over Laura's hair. "So pretty, Mama," she said.

Laura felt the tears form and told herself to stop being a damn sap. "Thank you, baby. Are you ready to go visit Uncle John?"

Chloe's sky-blue eyes sparkled as she nodded. They were so like Adam's that sometimes Laura shivered at the similarity. Whenever she thought of him, which was way more often than she damn well should, she was extremely thankful their daughter had his eyes, if only so she could have that one small part of him. Standing, she shook her head to rid it of the pining thoughts. They had no place in the life she'd created with Chloe and she needed to remember that.

Once they were dressed and bags packed with necessities for the day, they navigated to the subway and headed to Brooklyn. Chloe was a sponge, asking a multitude of questions about everything she saw along the way. It was amazing to Laura how quickly her mind churned. The way a three-year-old saw the world was simple and complex, all at the same time. It opened Laura's eyes to so many things and she was extremely grateful for the gift of her daughter.

As Chloe played with her tablet and the train chugged along, Laura's thoughts drifted to Adam again, as they so often did. Was he home? Had his deployment been seamless? She hoped with all her might he hadn't been injured or put in any sort of jeopardy.

She'd thought about tracking him down so many times. After all, even though his number had been destroyed in the worst coffee spill failure ever, she did know his last name. If she'd wanted to hire a private investigator, she could have. Chewing her lip as she stroked Chloe's hair, she let the guilt churn inside, knowing she didn't deserve a reprieve. He was a good man. Laura firmly believed that from their brief time together. He would make an excellent father and she was denying both him and Chloe by keeping them apart.

She'd been struggling with the guilt for some time now. Kayla and Joy had both made their positions clear: they believed she should track Adam down and tell him he had a daughter. Staring down at the child she loved immeasurably, she admitted the truth: she was terrified to locate Adam and tell him. What if he was angry at her deception? Would he sue her for custody? Would he take her baby away from her? Petrified at the thought, she clutched onto her decision to keep her secret. Even with the knowledge that it was terribly wrong. Shame burned in her gut as she drowned in the heavy emotion.

And if she was honest, there was another fear buried in the far reaches of her mind. A fear she'd somehow given her heart to Adam during their one night together and it had never quite been the same. If she analyzed the sentiment rationally, it seemed impossible. Her practical mind knew that. But she hadn't dated or slept with anyone since their evening together. She just didn't have the desire. Of course, being pregnant and raising a newborn didn't equate to a thriving dating life, but Laura had enjoyed sex when she'd been single and untethered. Now? She had absolutely no desire to sleep with anyone.

*Except for Adam.*

The words filtered through her mind before she could stop them, and they were true. So many nights she'd stared at the ceiling, remembering their fervent coupling. The way he'd stared into her eyes as his tongue swept over her most sensitive place. The way they'd laughed together and eaten pizza on the bed as if it were the most comfortable thing in the world. God, she yearned for that night. Laura wished so vehemently that he would hold her in his strong embrace once more. Lost to the swirling feelings, she didn't feel her daughter tug on her sleeve until it was almost too late.

"Mommy?" she said. "Are you sad?"

"No, baby," she said, noticing they were approaching their stop. Good grief. She'd been so stuck in false dreams that she'd almost missed the exit. Gathering their things, they headed up the stairs and onto the street under the bright summer sun.

Chloe held her hand as they walked to the cemetery. Navigating through the rows of white headstones, they came upon her brother's, situated in between all the other heroes who had valiantly given their lives for the freedom of others.

Spreading the blanket on the grass, they sat, Laura drawing Chloe close to sit on her lap. "Well, hello, Uncle John," she said, kissing Chloe's temple. "It's your favorite sister and your adorable as heck niece. How are you today?"

The birds chirped in the trees that lined the cemetery and a light breeze ruffled their hair. Chloe played with a dandelion she'd plucked as Laura contemplated John's grave. Still, after all these years, she missed him terribly. Content to sit in silence and remember her love for her brother, she didn't hear the footsteps crunch in the grass until they were directly behind her. Sensing a presence at her back, she turned to stare at the man who loomed above.

"Adam?" she whispered, lifting her hand to shield the sun from her eyes.

Chloe stared up as well, mouth open as she studied him.

The man who consumed so many of her thoughts stared at her daughter and then his gaze locked with hers—and it was filled with considerable anger.

# Chapter 9

♥

Adam started down at the striking woman who'd plagued his thoughts for the past four years and the little girl who shared his eyes. The resemblance was undeniable and Adam knew with every fiber in his body that this was his child. Stunned beyond belief, the words filtered through his mind. *I have a daughter.* Overwhelmed, he couldn't stop the emotions from churning within.

Shock. Disbelief. An instant heart tug toward the little girl who gaped up at him. And anger. God, he was angry. Nostrils flaring, he glared at Laura, not understanding how she could have betrayed him so vehemently.

She shuffled atop the blanket and stood, lifting the child to balance on her hip. Her deep hazel eyes were filled with sorrow and shame—and a latent fear. Tamping down his fury, he struggled with what to say.

"Chloe, this is Mommy's friend Adam. Can you say hello?"

"Hello, Adam." Her sweet voice sent a jolt of pure love directly into his pounding heart.

"Hello, Chloe. It's really nice to meet you. What a pretty dress you have."

She beamed, her tiny teeth adorable between her small lips. "I picked it out. It has butterflies."

Tears stung his eyes as he cleared his throat. "That it does. They're very cute." Training his gaze on Laura, he was impressed she faced him without reservation, chin high. "You promised, Laura," he said, his voice gravelly with emotion.

"I know," she whispered, wiping away the tear that escaped her eye. "It's...unforgivable. I'll discuss everything with you and talk as long as you want, but not here. Not in front of her. Please, Adam."

Part of him wanted to tell her to go to hell. How could the woman who'd captured his heart all those years ago be capable of such deception? Realizing the best way to find out was to allow himself the opportunity to ask her, he nodded. "Okay. We'll sit down and talk, but I'm reeling here, Laura. I just don't understand how you could keep this from me."

Her throat bobbed as she swallowed. "I know. I deserve your anger and your hate. I hate myself for so many choices I've made. I'll give you the opportunity to curse me out until your throat is raw, I swear. But we need to do it in private. When can you meet?"

Inhaling, he ran his hand through his hair. "I'm staying with my brother for a while. He lives on the Upper West Side. I retired from the navy a few months ago when I returned from my deployment. I'm on inactive reserve now and am contemplating applying to the New York State Reserve Corps. Aaron and Erika have two kids and I want to be around while they grow up. Since I was here, I decided to look you up. I didn't know your last name or have your number, but you told me you come here every July third so, here I am." He shrugged, the gesture relaying his overall frustration.

"Okay," she said, nodding. "My friends and I are having our annual July fourth cookout tomorrow on my roof deck.

They'll be able to watch Chloe while we talk. We can discuss everything in my apartment and I'll allow you to rail at me all you want."

There was such contrition in her expression that he almost believed she genuinely felt sorry for her duplicity. "All right," he said, gaze trailing to his daughter. His *daughter*. Holy shit. Reluctant to leave her, he asked, "Can I sit with you guys for a while?"

Laura appeared shocked. "I...um, yes, if you want to. We usually just come here and talk to Uncle John. Isn't that right, baby?"

Chloe nodded, her grin so cute that he was pretty sure his heart shattered in his chest. "I sing to Uncle John. 'Twinkle Twinkle'. You can sing with me."

"I'd love that, Chloe."

"Come on," Laura said, lowering back to the blanket. "Have a seat. It's a gorgeous day. We might as well enjoy it before you murder me."

Adam's lips twitched as he realized she still had her snarky sense of humor. Crouching beside them, he proceeded to spend his first moments with his daughter under the blazing summer sky.

Two hours later, Adam exited the subway and began trailing toward his brother's apartment. Lost in thought, he contemplated the steps that had led him here. His deployment to Afghanistan was long and arduous. He and his Navy SEAL team had been assigned several top ISIS and Taliban targets for capture and he'd been deployed for three and a half years until they all were in custody. It was grueling work in squalid desert conditions and he'd missed home terribly.

Two things maintained his morale: the sparse letters from his brother, informing him of the births of his niece and nephew, and thoughts of Laura. Striding along the gray sidewalk, he recalled how often he'd thought of her. Even though they'd only shared one night, something had shifted in his soul when she'd gazed up from the pillow, the poignant tear slipping down her cheek. He'd wiped it away, memorizing the softness of her skin, and realized that although it made absolutely no sense, he felt inherently connected to her after their intimate and passionate night together.

As the weeks wore on, he awaited her call, hoping she'd contact him and tell him she was pregnant. It was insane—Adam knew this—but it was the only way he knew how to reconnect with her since he didn't have her contact information or know her last name. Many times, under the bright desert moon, he'd berate himself for being an idiot. Who wished for something so complicated and impossible? But it was there, a pulsing need inside him, driving him to finish his mission so he could find her again.

Eventually, enough time passed that he realized she must've moved on. Was she with someone new? A man who could give her all the passion and love someone as gorgeous and magnificent as she deserved? Adam hoped so, although it burned, for he wanted to be the one to give her those things. So many times, he dreamed of her, running toward him as he returned home, smothering him in kisses and begging him to build a life with her. It was completely nonsensical and so out of character for his practical demeanor, but the thoughts lingered anyway.

When he'd returned home in February, he'd retired from his unit and gone on inactive reserve. Wanting to move closer to Aaron and Erika, he sold his condo in Washington DC and moved in with them in early June. They had a spare bedroom and his brother informed him that he was happy to host him in exchange for babysitting duty and help renovating the home office. Adam was more than happy to oblige. It allowed him to spend time with his niece and nephew and have a place to stay for a few months while he contemplated his next steps.

And it also brought him closer to Laura. He'd be lying if he claimed he didn't ache to find her. Although he was sure she was settled with someone by now, the desire to know for sure blazed in his gut. Determined to resolve it, he decided he would approach her when she visited her brother's grave in July. It was the only way he knew how to locate her, and probably reeked of desperation, but he just didn't give a damn. She was absolutely incredible and if he had even a small shot of finding her single and available, he had to try.

As he'd walked along the white headstones, he'd seen her dark hair fluttering in the breeze. She held a child on her lap and he'd wondered if that meant she was married. He'd approached slowly, not wanting to startle them, and then she'd turned and the girl had trained her gaze on his. It didn't take long to do the math. The child appeared to be around three years old and her eyes were the same ones he saw in the mirror every day. Immediately, he'd known she was his.

Anger welled within as he remembered Laura's hushed words, promising she would contact him if she was pregnant. Why hadn't she? What could've spurred her to hide his child from him? God, he'd missed so much. Her first steps. Her first words. What about the day she'd been born? Who had supported Laura through that?

Although it would've been impossible for him to return home due to his deployment, it still rankled him. He could've at least video-conferenced them, if only sporadically, and sent Laura letters of support and encouragement. He could've also sent money to ease any financial burdens of bringing a child into the world as a single parent. Frustrated he'd been denied those things, the anger stewed.

Remembering his time with Chloe today, the irritation migrated to newly formed, unwavering love. He'd sat with them at John's grave, singing songs with her that he sang with his brother's kids. She was a happy child who smiled freely and was precocious and talkative. Even with his frustration at Laura, he could admit from the brief hours they'd shared that she was raising their child to be a wonderful, loving little girl.

Tomorrow he would confront the woman who consumed his swirling thoughts. There were so many unanswered questions he was desperate to ask. Stalking up the front stairs of his brother's townhome, he opened the door and was greeted with an energetic scamp.

"Uncle Adam," Christina cried. "Where have you been?"

"I went to visit a friend," he said, lifting her and kissing her cheek. "Are you having fun with Dad today?"

She nodded. "Harry is sleeping and Daddy says I have to be quiet but it's boring. I want to play."

"A sleeping baby is a magical thing, kid," Adam said, setting her down. "I'm with your dad on that one. Let me talk to him for a few minutes and I'll play with you, okay?"

Excitement lit her blue eyes as she nodded. She scampered down the hallway and Adam went in search of his brother, finding him in the kitchen.

"How did it go?" Aaron asked, wiping down the counter, most likely from Christina's afternoon snack.

Blowing out a breath between puffed cheeks, Adam slid onto one of the stools at the island counter. "Holy shit, bro."

"That bad?" Aaron asked, arching a brow.

Adam rubbed his neck. "She has a kid, Aaron."

"Damn," his brother said, shaking his head. "That sucks. I know you were hoping she was still single."

"The thing is, she is single." Running his hand through his hair, he sighed. "The kid is mine, bro."

Aaron froze, the damp rag in his hand dangling as his mouth fell open. "What?"

"A little girl," Adam said, feeling his lips curve. "Chloe. She's the cutest damn thing I've ever seen."

His brother rested his palms on the counter, floored. "Are you sure?"

"Yes. She confirmed it and our resemblance is unmistakable. She has my eyes. *Our* eyes. *Fuck*," he whispered, rubbing his forehead. "I just never imagined she wouldn't contact me."

"Why didn't she?" Aaron asked, resentment in his tone. "That's awful."

Expelling a breath, he studied the marble counter. "I don't know. We're meeting to discuss tomorrow."

"We have the picnic tomorrow at the park."

"I know. I told Laura I'd meet her at three o'clock so I can spend the day with you guys. We're going to meet at her apartment and her friends are going to watch Chloe while we talk privately."

"Damn," Aaron said, lowering onto the stool beside him. "That's just...insane. Wow. You have a daughter."

"It's unbelievable. I'm still in shock. Of course, now my mind is reeling with what the next steps should be. Since you're my free attorney, I need your advice."

His brother chuckled. "Always love the family pro bono work. The first legal question you need to answer is if you want to file for custody. You can file for full or partial. If you want to do that, let me know and I'll prepare the paperwork. It usually takes about a month after filing for the summons to be served."

"Okay," Adam said, beleaguered by how vastly his life had changed in the span of a few hours. "I definitely want partial custody. I don't want to take her away from Laura but I want the legal right to see her and raise her."

"Then I suggest you let me file for partial custody this week. I'll prepare the paperwork and you'll have to sign it and get a paternity test."

Adam nodded. "I'll discuss with Laura tomorrow too. I hope she won't fight me on seeing Chloe. I'm not an absentee father, Aaron. I took one look at her and fell in love on the spot. I want to be a part of her life in every way."

"Then we'll make it happen," Aaron said with a tilt of his head. "And you're right that the process will be smoother if Laura is on board and you two have an amicable relationship."

"I'm so fucking pissed at her but she also seemed genuinely sorry that she didn't tell me. It was all over her face, which is still too damn gorgeous for words. Makes it that much harder for me to hate her."

"Are you still attracted to her?"

Standing, Adam lifted his hands in defeat. "Honestly, I think I'd still want her even if she intentionally unleashed the hounds of hell over Manhattan.  I can lie to myself and say it isn't true, but what's the point?  I pined for her for years, bro."

"What a cluster," his brother said, standing and walking over to pat his shoulder.  "You've really stepped in it, haven't you?"

"All the damn way," Adam said, breathing a laugh.  "I told Christina I'd play with her before I get to work on the far wall in the office."

"You're going to be an amazing father, Adam.  I'm so happy for you."

"Thanks," he said, hugging his brother and patting him on the back.  "I hope so."  Releasing him, Adam headed to find his niece and hopefully take his mind off the swirling revelations of the day, if only for a short while.

# Chapter 10

♥

Laura sat at the wooden picnic table beside one of the grills that lined the rooftop of her Manhattan condo building. Nervously tapping her foot, her eyes were glued to the door, awaiting Adam's arrival.

"Sweetie, I think you're going to hammer a hole in the floor. Your leg is twitching a mile a minute."

Laura looked at Joy and then down at her thigh, bare beneath her jean cut-off shorts. Yep, it was moving uncontrollably. "I can't stop, J. There are so many thoughts swirling through my mind. What if this gets ugly? What if he tries to take my baby?"

"Stop it, Laura," Kayla said, reaching over and grabbing her wrist as it sat atop the table. "You've told us numerous times over the past four years that Adam is an amazing guy who you felt so connected to the night you met. You're a fantastic judge of character and I can't imagine you'd be intimate with someone capable of taking a child away from their mother."

"It's no less than I deserve," she said, clenching her jaw. "You two kept telling me to track him down and I kept putting it off. I was so afraid that this exact scenario was going to happen. Now I'm screwed."

"You need to give him the benefit of the doubt, sweetie, just as you want him to do with you. Once you explain what happened, he's going to understand how this situation organically evolved. I know it."

"I hope so," she said, biting her lip. "It doesn't help that he's even more gorgeous than when he left. I mean, who in the hell ages backward? I almost swallowed my tongue when I saw him yesterday. He's hands-down the hottest guy I've ever been with."

Kayla smiled. "Well, then, it makes sense why Chloe is so beautiful. I can't wait to meet this hunk of a man. You've talked about him for years. It's about damn time."

"I have wieners for everyone and an extra one for you," Carter said, winking at Kayla as he sat down the tray of hot dogs, fresh from the grill.

Kayla wrinkled her nose. "Gross. There are children present."

"George thinks I'm hilarious. Right, George?"

Joy's five-year-old nodded and snickered. "I love wieners."

"You're officially fired from babysitting duty," Joy said, running her fingers through her son's hair. "Do you want ketchup, sweetheart?" George nodded and she set about preparing a hot dog for him.

Laura's phone rang and she answered it, swallowing thickly as she spoke terse words to the doorman. "He's on his way up."

"You're strong, Laura," Kayla said, rubbing her back. "You can do this. Remember to be patient and compassionate. It's better if you two get along while you work this out."

Laura nodded and rubbed her wet palms on her thighs. The concrete door creaked open and Adam stepped onto the roof. He was so handsome in his khaki shorts, sneakers, and t-shirt, which showcased his rippling muscles underneath. Longing rushed through her as she remembered clutching his broad shoulders as he'd pummeled her in the shower and spoken dirty, reverent words in her ear. It had been one of the most erotic moments of her life.

His gaze found hers and he began trailing toward them. Chloe ran up beside her, tugging her shirt and whispering, "Adam is here."

"I know," she said, running her palm over her daughter's ponytail. "I asked him to come by. We're going to go talk while you stay here and play with everyone, okay?" Chloe nodded and turned to stare up at Adam.

"Hi," he said to Laura and then crouched down to eye-level with Chloe. "Hey, Chloe. Great to see you again. I told my brother how much fun we had singing yesterday."

Chloe smiled, swaying back and forth as she regarded him. "'Twinkle Twinkle' is my favorite."

He squinted, pretending to ponder. "I like 'The Wheels on the Bus' but 'Twinkle Twinkle' is pretty cool too."

"Hey, man," Carter said, approaching him, hand outstretched. "Carter Manheim. Nice to finally meet you. Laura's told us great things. This is my wife, Kayla, our sons, Liam and Charlie, Sam, Joy, George and their baby, Jacqueline, who's passed out in the stroller over there."

Adam shook Carter's hand and waved to everyone. "Really nice to meet you all. Laura told me so much about you the night we met."

"We're a ragtag family here, so that's nice to hear," Kayla said. "We're very protective of each other and we love Laura to pieces. We're excited you agreed to come here today, Adam, and hope you'll listen with an open heart when Laura explains the circumstances of the past few years."

"Okay," Laura said, standing. Arching a brow, she said to Adam, "My friend is trying to tell you that if you're a jerk or threaten me in any way, she'll kick your ass. It's sweet, but I don't need anyone to fight my battles. I'm a big girl.

We can head to my place to talk but do you want anything first? Carter just made hot dogs and we've got some chips and veggies."

"I'm good," Adam said, his tone unreadable. "I think I'd just rather get to it."

"All right. Guys," she said, turning to face the table, "take care of my little munchkin. I'll see you in a bit."

Straightening her spine, she steeled herself for what would most likely be one of the most difficult discussions of her life. "Follow me." Head held high, she led Adam to her apartment.

Adam followed Laura down the hallway, unable to move his gaze from the sway of her hips in the sexy-as-hell shorts. Those long legs he'd caressed the night they'd loved each other stretched beneath the fabric to the cute sandals she wore. A tight tank top showcased her breasts, which seemed a bit larger than he'd remembered when he'd glanced at them on the roof. Was that due to her pregnancy with Chloe? Her hair fell straight to her shoulders, glossy and silky, and he imagined having it trail over his thigh as she took him in her mouth. Feeling himself harden, he pushed the thoughts away to focus on the task at hand.

Once inside, she closed the door and headed to the fridge to grab two beers. Popping them open, she handed him one. "I think we need alcohol for this."

Taking it, he gave her a wayward grin. "Damn straight." Lifting the bottle, he clinked it with hers. "To Chloe."

"To Chloe," she said, eyes locked with his as she imbibed a huge gulp. Gesturing with her head to the couch, he followed her there and sat. Not even pretending to know how to open the conversation, he waited for her to speak.

Inhaling deeply, she set her beer on the coffee table and rubbed her palms over her thighs. Latching her gaze to his, she said, "So, um, yeah. I didn't take the morning-after pill."

The situation was so uncomfortable that a laugh escaped his throat. "I pretty much figured that out, Laura."

"I had every intention of doing it when I got home that morning," she said, palms lifting in a shrug. "But Sam showed up at my hotel door and informed me that Kayla and Carter had been in a terrible car accident."

His eyebrows drew together. "How terrible?"

"They're fine now but, that day, we had no idea if Carter was going to make it. Kayla was banged up pretty bad and he was on life support. It was touch and go for a while and we all rushed straight to the hospital. I didn't get home until Sunday night. I was so exhausted that I fell asleep and finally went to the pharmacy on Monday morning to get the pill."

"Okay," he said, taking a sip of his beer. "And did you take it then?"

She chewed her bottom lip before answering. "No. I came home and fiddled with the box in my bathroom. Then, I did some serious reflection. The pharmacist told me that due to the time that had elapsed, the efficacy of the pill would be severely diminished. I contemplated for a while and decided I wasn't going to take it. And I'll never regret my decision, Adam. Chloe is the best thing that's ever happened to me. I'm extremely thankful I made that choice."

Setting the bottle on the table, he scooted closer to her. "I understand everything you're telling me, Laura. I just don't understand why you didn't call me when you realized you were pregnant. You made a promise to me and I'm extremely hurt you didn't contact me. I've lost so much time with her. It's incredibly unfair and I'm trying really hard not to scream here because I'm pretty fucking pissed that I have a daughter I knew nothing about."

Tears welled in her eyes and he told himself to remain strong. Although he wanted so badly to comfort her, she was in the wrong and needed to be held accountable for her actions.

"Be right back," she said, standing and plodding to the island. Reaching in her purse, she pulled out a notepad. Sauntering back over, she sat and handed it to him. "Take a look at this."

Adam took the pad, realizing it was the one he'd written his name and number on. The words were now faded and illegible except for his first name. It appeared that something had been spilled on the parchment.

"I'd gotten coffee from the lobby that morning and spilled it all over the damn pad when Sam knocked on my door. The paper soaked it up and your number bled into it until it was illegible. I know it sounds ridiculous, but that's truly what happened, Adam. I did try to find you on Facebook and Instagram but you weren't on there. I figured that with your clandestine assignment, you didn't have social media accounts."

"I didn't have much use for social media during deployment," he said, brow furrowing as he stared at the pad. "Erika's trying to get me to use Facebook more but I don't go on it much and my profile is private. It seems like a bunch of people complaining or posting selfies of activities that seem completely unwarranted of attention."

Laura laughed, her face transforming into something so beautiful. Yearning curled in his gut as he regarded her glossy lips and he told himself to chill. He was supposed to be grilling her, not lusting after her.

"Yep, social media is a bitch. I use it as sparingly as I can but it's a necessary evil sometimes."

"Did you ever think about hiring someone to track me down? There are tons of competent private investigators in Manhattan."

"I know," she said, stretching out her legs and shaking her head. "Kayla and Joy urged me to hire someone and find you but I just kept procrastinating."

Scooching closer, he encircled her wrist, noticing she stiffened slightly. "Why, Laura? Why would you keep this from me?"

Resting her head in her free hand, she shook it, hair swishing as her lips compressed. "It was so selfish, Adam. I was sure you were going to find out and be so pissed. And then I became terrified you'd try to take her away." Lifting those gorgeous eyes to his, they swam with sincerity. "She's all I have. My entire life. If I lose her, I don't know how I'll go on."

There was a sadness to the words, causing Adam's heart to constrict. "I understand your fear, Laura, but you denied me the chance to know my little girl. It's breaking my heart."

A sob tore from her throat as she moved toward him. Ever so slowly, she palmed his cheek as tears swam in her eyes. "I realize that now. It was such an awful thing to do. I feel terrible, Adam. I'm so sorry."

Hating that the woman he felt so drawn to had wronged him so deeply, he slid his hand over her jaw. "I'm so fucking angry at you, kitten," he said, calling her by the reverent nickname he still fondly remembered.

"I understand," she said, the tears starting to fall down her cheeks. "I'd hate me if I were you. It's unforgivable. There were obstacles in the way of me finding you but I should've tried harder. Not only did I deny you, but I denied Chloe from getting to know you. It's a terrible misstep on my part. You're such a good man. Even though we only spent one night together, I felt it in my bones. I feel it now."

Gliding his other hand around the back of her head, he rested his forehead against hers. "I won't let you keep her from me any longer, Laura. I want to be a part of her life. A father in every way."

"I want that too," she said, her voice raw. "I hope one day you can forgive me. I missed you so much, Adam. I thought about you all the time. The day she was born and had your eyes, I knew I was screwed."

His lips formed a warbled smiled as his thumb traced over her lip. "And why was that?"

"Because it meant I'd think of you more than I already did, which was pretty much all the damn time."

Adam held her, elated by her words, thrilled at how her body trembled against him. "Show me," he whispered.

"Adam…"

"Show me, kitten," he said, softly brushing his lips against hers.

Her body shuddered and then she broke, entwining her arms around his neck and cementing her lips to his. Plying them open, her tongue darted inside, searching to find his, mewling when they met and slid over each other. Starving from the drought of not having her for so long, he kissed her back, showing her with his skilled tongue how much he'd pined for her too. Threading his fingers through her hair, his tongue warred with hers as she slid over his lap.

Pushing him to lie on his back, she glided over him, straddling him as she continued the fervent kiss. Her mouth moved over him, desperate and filled with desire, and his hand slid down her body to cup the mound of her ass. Clutching the tight globe, he jutted his erection into the juncture of her thighs, craving contact with her sweet body after being denied so long.  She moaned, retracting her tongue to nibble his lips before lifting her head to look into his eyes.

"I convinced myself I'd never get to kiss you again," she whispered, trailing her fingers over his cheek. "I've dreamed of it for years."

His hands cupped her face as he stared at her.  Swollen lips sat below reddened cheeks and eyes glassy with desire.  Oh, how he'd ached to see her just like this for so very long.

"My mind is telling me I'm supposed to be mad as hell at you, Laura, but it's really hard when you look at me like that. You're so fucking beautiful."

A flush swept over her face causing his body to harden further. "Looks like we still have our undeniable chemistry, my friend.  I've rarely felt it for someone as much as I feel it for you."

His irises darted between hers. "How is that going to work while we navigate this extremely complicated situation?"

The corner of her sexy lips curved. "We could just fuck like rabbits every time we need to negotiate.  It seems the most enjoyable solution by far."

Chuckling, he threaded his fingers through her hair. "As fun as that sounds, I think we need to take a more practical approach. Although my body hates me right now for saying that."

Giving him one last soft smile, she eased away to sit on the couch.  Rising to sit next to her, he reached for her hand, lacing his fingers through hers. "As upset and angry as I am, I don't want to fight with you, Laura.  Us being at odds won't help Chloe.  My brother is a lawyer and has offered to help me navigate this with you."

"Kayla is a lawyer too and has offered the same." Squeezing his fingers, she said, "I don't want to fight with you either. You have every right to hate me and I'm humbled you're willing to tackle this situation practically. It's way more than I deserve."

"Look, Laura, I get it. From what you've just told me, there were a lot of mitigating factors after I left that morning. It was a lot for anyone to handle and you did the best you could. It's a waste of energy for me to fight you tooth and nail. I want this to be amicable. But I also want to be clear: I want partial custody of Chloe. She's my daughter and I intend to raise her as my own."

Her color-flecked eyes darted over his face as she studied him. "You deserve that. It terrifies me because she's all I have, but I won't deny you that, Adam. If you want to file for partial custody, I'm on board. In the meantime, we'll set up a visitation schedule so you can spend time with her. How long are you planning on being in New York?"

"Honestly, with this recent turn of events, I'm probably going to move here. I'll start looking for an apartment tomorrow and will apply to the New York Navy Reserve Corps. Their headquarters are in the Bronx so it's pretty convenient."

"Okay," she said, her gaze falling to the ground.

She looked so forlorn that he slid his fingers under her chin and lifted it. "What is it?"

She gave a dejected shrug. "I don't want to share her. It's my own shit so don't give it a second thought. I have to deal with it on my own. It's no less than I deserve."

"I don't want to take her away from you, Laura. I just want to help you raise her and be her father."

"I know," she whispered, the now-familiar sadness crossing her features. "It's just hard." Standing, she tugged her hand from his and sliced it through the air. "Enough of the pity party. It's annoying. I think we should discuss next steps and write them down so we have a firm plan."

"I'm on board," he said. "Let's do it."

Grabbing the notebook from the nearby table, she sat down and they got to work planning the next chapter of their lives.

# Chapter 11

Over the next hour, they planned the basics. Laura always scheduled her personal styling appointments each week on Mondays, Wednesdays, and Thursdays. On those days, Chloe was enrolled in daycare. The other days of the week were left open for Laura to spend with her daughter.

"How's the business going, by the way?" Adam asked.

"Good. It's nice to do it part-time and I'm loaded now that I've inherited my trust. It allows me to spend so much time with her. I'm extremely lucky."

"I want to contribute financially too, Laura," he said, his tone firm. "It's important for me to support Chloe and I want to give you child support as well, for her clothes, food, and other essentials."

Her lips curved into a grin. "That's such a generous offer, Adam, but I honestly don't need it. I consider my inheritance a sort of cosmic karma for having to deal with my mother. I have more money than I'll ever need. It's unnecessary but very much appreciated."

"It's non-negotiable, Laura. I aim to do my part here."

"Adam—"

"Non-negotiable," he interrupted, holding up his hand.

"Okay," she said, shrugging. "If you want to contribute money, go ahead. It's really admirable. Thank you."

His gaze fell to the floor as worry pervaded his muscles.

"What's wrong?"

Lifting his eyes to hers, he asked, "What if she doesn't understand? Should I ask her to call me 'Dad'? What did you tell her about her father?"

She compressed her lips, contemplating before answering. "Thankfully, she's still too young to ask too many questions. Sometimes she asks me why George and the twins have daddies while she doesn't. I usually just tell her that she's so special and has so many people who love her that she doesn't need just one daddy." Her gaze trailed to her clenched hands in her lap, her posture indicating she wanted to say more.

"And what else?" he asked.

"Nothing," she said, waving her hand. "She seems to accept that for now. I think that after you've gotten to know her a bit, we can move forward slowly and tell her you're her dad. If that works for you."

"I have no idea how to be a parent, so I'll defer to you on this, Laura. If that's what you think is right, that's what we'll do."

Her expression was so genuine as she spoke. "You're going to be an incredible father. I'm so grateful, Adam. Thank you."

"We'll see," he said, winking. "Don't extoll my virtues yet. I might suck."

"No way," she said, grinning as she consulted the notepad. "Okay, so you're going to have her every Saturday, Monday, and Thursday for now. How much longer will you wait before applying to the local reserve corps?"

"I have enough saved from selling my condo to remain on inactive duty for over a year. I'd like to spend that time with

Chloe. I'll most likely apply early next year. By then, we'll hopefully be more settled and have a set schedule."

"Okay. This might rub you the wrong way, and I certainly don't want it to, but if you want to take more time off, I'd be happy to cover your expenses. It's the least I can do for how awesome you're being about this entire situation."

"Thanks, but I'm too proud to take your charity, Laura."

"It's not charity. You're the father of my child, Adam. You've given me such a gift. One that I'll never be able to repay you for and is incredibly important to me. Anything I have is yours. I won't force you," she said, holding up her hand when he opened his mouth to argue, "but the offer's always open. That's the last we'll speak of it unless you bring it up."

"Sweetheart," he said, lifting her hand and placing a soft kiss on the back, "that's incredibly generous but I'd never take your money. I'm appreciative you're not fighting me on the custody. We're both dedicated to making this work."

"I'm so glad we are," she said, squeezing his hand. "It's up to you if you want to file with the courts, Adam. As far as I'm concerned, we can just as easily figure this out without government interference. I can have Kayla draw up a contract that details the visitation, child support you insist on paying," she gave him a teasing eye roll, "and all the other things we agree on. But it's totally up to you. I want you to feel comfortable. I know I'm probably not high on your *trustworthy* list right now." She made quotation marks with her fingers, emphasizing the word.

Weighing her words, Adam realized he did trust her. She relayed a genuineness and straightforwardness in every discussion they'd had so far. After hearing the details of what happened once he left after the night they spent together, he better understood the choices she'd made. Humans were flawed creatures and she'd done the best she could. Yes, she'd fucked up along the way, not making a true effort to find him, but he'd been almost unreachable and would've only been able to have minimal contact at best. In the end, it would've been an impossible situation no matter what, and she'd navigated it the best way she knew how. After a long deliberation, he nodded.

"Okay. Have Kayla draw up the papers and I'll have my brother look over them. I'll probably want to file for formal custody eventually, but I realize that will drag Chloe into court and require supervised visits and all sorts of other things. I should probably figure out how to be a father first and then go down the formal road of seeking custody. Let's start off informally and reassess after a few months."

"Thank you," she whispered, sliding her hand over his knee. The motion drove him crazy and he struggled to tamp down his arousal. "I'll do better with my promises this time. You deserve that."

Standing, he drew her to her feet and into a warm embrace. Running his hand over her back, he inhaled her fragrant hair. Thrilled to be holding her again, he placed his lips on the shell of her ear. "What are we going to do about the fact that we still want each other?"

She shivered, resting her forehead on his chest. "I have no fucking idea."

They swayed together, the weight of their mutual attraction between them. Finally, he murmured, "Let's take it day by day. But I'm not a bullshitter, Laura. I still want you badly. I think it's only a matter of time before we end up back in bed together. My only worry is that things might get messy."

Drawing back, she gazed into his soul. "I'm worried too. I experience a lot of feelings around you, Adam."

Eyes searching hers, he nodded. "We'll do our best, then. Whatever comes our way."

"I mean, you did say you'd love to date me, all those years ago. You could ask a sister out, once things have calmed down. I haven't had an adult night out in months. It's embarrassing." With a sardonic arch of her eyebrow, she disentangled from his embrace and gathered the empty beer bottles, walking them to the sink and rinsing them before placing them in the recycling bin. Striding over to her, he crossed his arms and leaned on the island counter.

"You haven't been on a date since having Chloe?"

Facing him, chin held high, she said in an almost regal tone, "Adam, I haven't been on a date or slept with anyone since I was with you." Giving a nod, she trailed to the front door, opening it wide. "Come on. Let's go hang with Chloe and my friends and you can get to know them a bit before you go home."

Adam stared at her, his heart pounding from the bomb she'd dropped. It was incredibly meaningful to him that she hadn't been with anyone since their night together all those years ago. The thought shifted something in his solar plexus, and he lifted his hand to rub his chest.

"Come on," she said, motioning to the hallway with her head. "Before we lose what's left of the sunlight."

Exhilarated by her stunning admission, he joined her and headed to the roof to spend time with his daughter.

Adam thoroughly enjoyed his time with Laura's "friend family," as she so lovingly called them. Carter was hilarious and extremely fun to be around and Kayla had a whip-smart sense of humor. Joy and Sam seemed to be the sweetest people on the planet and the children were all adorable.  Having spent time with Aaron's kids, especially recently, Adam really enjoyed hanging with the little tykes.

Chloe dragged out a bucket of sidewalk chalk from the children's play area in the corner of the rooftop and he proceeded to sit with her and draw on the cemented surface for what seemed like hours.  The chalk was enormous in her hand and her tiny tongue would stick out as she concentrated on coloring.  Her drawings were a delightful mess and he colored along with her, enthralled by how she directed him.  Filled with pride, he decided she was a leader and would become President one day.  Yep, that sounded about right.

Glancing up, he noticed Laura gazing at them, chin resting on her fist as she sat at the picnic table.  She smiled wistfully and he waved, giving her a quick wink.  She was gorgeous in the waning light of the sun as it set behind the large buildings.  Those long legs seemed to shimmer, causing him to imagine running his tongue over every dip and hollow.  The thought of nuzzling the back of her knee made him so hard that he thought he might burst.  Reminding himself that children were present, he attempted to focus on the boring sidewalk chalk.

Her admission had stunned him.  How could someone as beautiful and sexually forward as Laura remain abstinent for four years?  His mind drifted to the handful of women he'd lain with during his deployment. They'd all been on various bases he visited, all of them used to sleeping with the soldiers who trailed through.  His trysts with them had been brief and untethered.  Those were the types of intimacies he was used to.  But now he was free of the constant deployments.  Free to build something more permanent in his life.  Would it be possible to build that with Laura?  To create something with her and Chloe that was all their own?

Although he'd lain with a few women over the past few years, Laura's face has been the one emblazoned in his mind.  He thought of her so often he sometimes thought he'd gone mad, clutching onto something that was supposed to only last for one night.  Smiling at his daughter as she sat beside him, concentrating with all her might on coloring the concrete blue, he realized he must've known somewhere deep within.  Must've sensed that his incredibly passionate and meaningful night with Laura would lead to more. Feeling extremely lucky, he gazed at her, blood pounding in his veins as she threw back her head and laughed at something Kayla said.  Filled with a pulsing desire to be the one who made her laugh that jubilantly, he committed to exploring his feelings for her. After all, she'd told him to ask her on a date, and once he'd spent some time with Chloe, he intended to do just that.

Night eventually fell and everyone packed up and headed home.  Laura offered for Adam to read to Chloe, spurring excitement in his chest. Together they helped her get ready for bed so Adam could learn her routine.  Once she was dressed in adorable pajamas adorned with tiny rockets and stars, she picked two books from the shelf and climbed under the covers.  Laura draped across the foot of her bed while Adam held her to his chest, reading the books with thick, cardboard-like pages.  Once both books were done, and her eyes were drooping, he stood and placed a kiss on her forehead.

"Goodnight, Chloe."

"Goodnight, Adam.  I'm glad you're Mommy's friend."

"Me too, sweetheart," he said, unable to explain how his heart had expanded a thousand times wider in his chest.

Rubbing it, he brushed her hair from her temples.  "Sweet dreams."

"Good night, baby," Laura said, bending over and placing a kiss on her lips.  The gesture was poignant and turned Adam's already decimated heart to mush.  A swell of protectiveness swept over him and in that moment, he knew he'd die to protect either one of them from harm.  Following Laura from the room, he switched off the light and they headed to the kitchen.

"Well, you survived your first day as a dad," she said, beaming.  "Well done, sir."  She gave him a good-natured salute.

"It was incredible, Laura.  Thank you.  I'm overwhelmed by her.  She's amazing."

"She is," was her soft reply.

"We're going to kick ass at this.  I know it."

"Me too."  Stretching her arms above her head, she yawned. Her breasts strained beneath the tight tank top, causing his mouth to turn dry as sandpaper.  He could still remember the texture of her pebbled nipples against his tongue, all these years later, and yearned to suck them again.  *Soon*, he reminded himself, wanting to stay on task.  First, he would settle into a pattern with Chloe and get his life in New York settled.  Then, he would seduce the woman he'd pined for since leaving her all those years ago.  Heart full with possibility, he placed a gentle kiss on her forehead and exited the apartment, excited at what the future held.

<h1 style="text-align:center">Chapter 12</h1>

♥

Adam settled into a seamless rhythm with Chloe. The days he spent with her were comprised of playdates at the playground, walks around Central Park, meals at McDonald's and various other excursions. Although they might seem mundane to some, he enjoyed his time with his little girl immensely. They were forming a bond, and each time she smiled or laughed with him, he fell more in love with her. Never had he felt such joy from the simple actions of another. She was truly a blessing and he was extremely grateful to Laura for raising such a sweet, exceptional daughter.

She and Christina also got along fabulously, and his niece was happy to have a new friend to play with. Adam found an apartment only a few blocks from his brother and loved taking the girls to the playground that sat in the park at the end of the block. Their giggles would ring out over the open space, joyful and innocent.

Another perk of his new life was that he got to spend time with Laura. Getting to know her on a personal level only increased his attraction to her. Together, they would take Chloe on excursions to the park, museums or various other child-appropriate venues. It was a new world for Adam and

Laura took pity on him, eyes sparkling with laughter as she helped him navigate being a dad.

When he'd seen her all those years ago, the sexual attraction had been instant. It still burned deep in his gut and he wanted nothing more than to make love to her again. But, more than that, he realized what a generous and loving person she was. Laura always put Chloe first—even if it was to her detriment. There were times he noticed she forgot to eat dinner because Chloe needed a bath and that was higher on her list than her own nourishment. Or other instances when Chloe didn't feel well, causing Laura to cancel her client appointments without a second thought. Her selflessness with their daughter stirred something in Adam, increasing his growing admiration.

And she was gentle with him too. When he didn't understand how to fasten Chloe into the high chair that had about a thousand clasps for some frustrating reason, Laura was there guiding him. She would instruct him instead of doing it for him and it exemplified her willingness to teach him how to navigate being a father. She would sometimes direct him on heating food for Chloe before they ate the meals she prepared and chuckled when he was terrified it was too warm.

"You put the plate in for ten seconds, Adam," she said, one night, sparing him an amused glance. "The idea is to warm it, you know."

"I don't want her to burn her tongue," he'd said feeling himself pout.

"God, you're so cute when you frown like that," she said, winking at him and gesturing to the microwave. "Put it in for thirty seconds at least. We'll test it first before we give it to her. I promise it's fine."

He'd proceeded to heat the vegetables appropriately, feigning burning his mouth as he ate it. She and Chloe had broken out into joyful laughter, the sound so melodious. They were slowly forming a family unit and Adam realized that after all his years of being a nomad, he actually had the desire to put down permanent roots.

Sometimes, Adam questioned whether he should be shocked he felt so comfortable around Laura and Chloe. For some reason, their arrangement just worked. Perhaps he desired to make up for lost time; perhaps it was Laura's willingness to include him in their tiny circle. Whatever it was, he was extremely grateful.

Sometimes, as he waited for her to dress Chloe, he would pick up the framed pictures scattered around her living room. Several of them showed Laura when she was pregnant, as well as Chloe as a newborn. Reverently, he would trace his finger over Laura's extended belly in the images, wishing he'd been able to support her through her pregnancy. Then, his mind would drift to wistful yearnings...building something permanent with Laura and Chloe...having another baby with her so he could be by her side the entire time...marrying her and adopting Chloe as his own...

The sentiments were quite serious, but Adam had never shirked responsibility. He'd always wanted to settle down once he retired from active deployment. To find a wife and create a family. Could he have those things with Laura and Chloe? The idea filled him with hope and each day he spent with them, it rang truer in his heart.

The only drawback to his new arrangement was his brother's reaction to his agreement with Laura. Aaron thought it incredibly naïve and unwise for Adam not to formally file for custody. Sitting on the swing as he watched

Chloe and Christina play, he recalled their last argument on the subject.

"This is absurd, Adam," Aaron said, shaking the papers that Kayla had drawn up with forceful indignation. "This contract doesn't give you any legal rights in the courts. If Laura decides to run away with Chloe tomorrow, you're screwed."

"I trust her, Aaron," Adam said, hands situated on his hips as he seethed in frustration. "We've decided to go this route for now and I'd really appreciate your acceptance. If you can't give it, that's your deal, but I've made my decision."

His brother scoffed. "You trust the woman who kept your child secret from you for four years? That's just dumb, bro."

"Well, it's my life and I'd rather be an idiot who does this amicably with her than an asshole who scares the crap out of the mother of my child. She's terrified I'm going to take her away. I won't let her live with that fear, Aaron."

"You're playing with fire here, man. I'll look these over and notarize them when you sign, but I'm going to draw up the custody papers just in case. I think there will come a time when you'll need them. Trust me, I've done family law for years. These things rarely work out as planned."

"Drawing up a formal filing right now is futile. I've made my decision. Let me know when you look it over so I can sign it."

Annoyance flashed across his brother's expression before he stalked from the room.

Sighing, Adam clutched onto the chains of the swing, wishing they could see eye to eye on the matter. Sadly, it didn't seem possible. Firm in his trust of Laura, he vowed to move forward with their agreement.

"Uncle Adam!" a voice chimed, interrupting his thoughts. "Look what I found."

"Holy cow," he said, sliding from the swing and crouching down. "It's a caterpillar. How cute." He ran his finger over the soft pelt of the creature Christina held in her tiny fingers.

"Me too," Chloe said, holding it up so Adam could examine it. "They're best friends, like me and Chrissy."

"That's pretty darn adorable, sweetheart," he said, placing a kiss on her silky hair. "You two are my favorite best friends in the entire world."

"You can be our best friend too," Christina said.

"How about I race you for it? First one to the gate is the *best* best friend!" Grinning, he began running as they squealed behind him and tried to catch up, the caterpillars long forgotten. Reveling in their laughter, he dismissed the tension between him and Aaron. It would work out in the end. These things always did. Confident in that notion, he helped the kids expend some energy, knowing it would help their mothers ensure an early and seamless bedtime later that evening.

# Chapter 13

♥

Several weeks into his new life, Adam was ready to pursue Laura. He'd become enamored with the woman who was such a brilliant mother to his little girl. Being sexy as hell didn't hurt either. Each time he was around her, he almost drowned in the smell of her hair, the timbre of her laugh and the gentle way she squeezed his hand when she silently thanked him for something. She was a remarkable woman and his body buzzed in anticipation of getting to hold her while she moaned in his arms.

One night, after he'd finished reading to Chloe and tucked her in, he found her in the kitchen loading the dishwasher. She was bent over the appliance, the apple ripe globes of her ass almost bursting from her tight shorts. Blood surged to his shaft as he clenched his hands at his sides, dying to touch the luscious mounds.

"Chloe's in bed," he said, his voice gravelly.

"Sweet," she said, straightening. His face must've tightened because her lips turned into a grin. "Were you ogling my ass?"

Stalking toward her, he grasped her wrist and drew her into his straining body. Thrusting one hand in the hair at her nape, he clutched one of her ass cheeks with the other, reveling in her gasp as her body aligned with his.

"Yes, woman, I was ogling your ass. It's so fucking gorgeous. I don't think you even begin to comprehend how sexy you are."

Full lips curved as she slid her arms around his neck. "I have dried banana on my shirt and smell like a mom, but whatever floats your boat."

"You're perfect, Laura," he said, nuzzling her nose with his. "I wanted to give us time to settle into this thing but I need to spend some time with you. Just you. Let me take you to dinner on Saturday."

She bit her lip, the action so sexy his knees almost buckled. "I could probably get Kayla or Joy to watch Chloe."

"Yes," he said, nipping her lips. "Either or. As long as she can stay the night with them."

Her eyes widened. "Oh, you want to have a sleepover." She waggled her eyebrows. "Only big boys get to have sleepovers. Are you sure you're ready for that?"

"I'm so damn ready, kitten. Can't you feel how ready I am?" He jutted his erection into her abdomen, shivering as her breathing hitched.

"You seem pretty ready," she murmured. As she studied him, he sensed a slight hesitancy.

"Don't be scared, honey," he said, understanding this would drastically change their relationship. It was daunting but Adam refused to let their attraction remain unsated any longer.

"So much will change," she said, "once we sleep together. Are you ready for that, Adam? I'm not sure I am."

A sliver of hurt sliced through his chest. "Don't you trust me?" he asked, sliding his hand around to cup her jaw.

"More than anything," she said, lifting to her toes to brush a kiss across his lips. "I don't trust my own heart. I'm afraid it might fall for you too easily."

He could tell the admission was hard for her and wanted so badly to assure her. "My heart's pretty tied up in you too, Laura. I never told you how much I thought of you when I was gone. I think I was afraid to tell you, maybe because I wasn't ready, but you consumed my thoughts over there. You got me through so many long, lonely nights. My heart's been with you for a pretty long time."

Her resulting smile was so reverent. "Damn. You're good. That was very romantic, soldier."

"Just wait 'til I get started," he murmured against her lips. "There's more where that came from." Urging her lips open with his, he consumed her, open-mouthed and deep. Blood pulsed through his veins as he poured all the passion he felt for her into their fiery kiss. Unable to control his hips, he undulated into her quivering body, elated when she wrapped her leg around his waist, allowing him to seat his erection into the juncture of her core. Man, if they didn't have clothes on, he'd spread her across the island and fuck her so thoroughly. He wanted to claim her, mark her, so she understood how primal and intrinsic his desire was for her.

"Good grief," she moaned, head lolling back as her eyes remained closed. "I swear, you're the world's best kisser. If our daughter wasn't next door, I'd do so many naughty things to you right now."

His deep chuckle surrounded them. "Funny, I was just thinking the same thing." Tenderly brushing her hair from her face, he released her, noticing how their chests both heaved as they struggled to catch their breath.

"Okay," she said, grinning up at him. "You can take me on a date. Surprise me. I like to be wooed. If you show me a fantastic time, you might just get lucky."

"Hot damn," he said, winking.

"I'll make sure Chloe stays overnight with one of the ladies. This is going to be fun." Her eyebrows lifted in anticipation.

"Sure is, kitten." Leaning down, he gave her a peck on the lips. "See you in two days. I'll pick you up at seven. Wear something sexy."

"You're not digging the dried banana?" she teased, pointing at the stain on her tank top.

"Honey, I dig anything you wear. My favorite look is naked. We'll be sure to try that one after our date."

"Can't wait." Blowing him a kiss, she stood by the sink as he gave her a wave and exited. Unable to erase his perma-grin, Adam whistled almost the entire way home.

# *Chapter 14*

♥

Saturday rolled around and Laura felt extremely nervous. It was so unlike her since she was usually confident and fearless, but she felt it all the same. She hadn't been on a date in four long years. Hadn't felt the touch of a man on her skin in so very long. Her body was so different from when she'd first made love to Adam. Staring in the mirror, robe held open, she traced her fingers over the stretch marks that lined her hips. Above them, on her lower abdomen, sat her C-section scar. Would Adam think it ugly? Would he still want her?

Groaning, she closed the robe and pushed the maddening thoughts away. They'd do her no good and she wanted to have fun tonight. No, she damn well *deserved* to have fun tonight. Mustering every bit of confidence she had, she forged ahead with getting ready.

Chloe burst into the room, Joy, and Kayla behind her. "Mommy! I'm going to have a sleepover with Aunt Kayla and Aunt Joy."

"I know, baby," she said, stroking her hair as she stood at the bathroom counter. "It's going to be so fun."

"Mommy's going to have fun tonight too," Kayla said, leaning on the door frame, arms crossed as she waggled her eyebrows.

"We'll see," Laura muttered. "I haven't done this in a long time. I'm not sure my lady parts still work."

"Oh, you'll be fine," Joy said, entering the expansive bathroom and sliding to sit on the counter. "I'm so happy for you, Laura. Adam is amazing and he's so freaking handsome. I hope he whisks you off your feet and gives you the fairy tale ending you deserve."

"I can always count on you to make everyone's life into a rom-com with a happy ending, J." Picking up the palette, she began applying eye shadow. "What are you guys going to do tonight?"

"We're going to hang at my house since Carter's working. His play only has two more weeks and then we get a much-needed vacation. Thank god."

"You guys never got to go on your honeymoon," Laura said, swiping the powder over her lids. "It's about time."

"I'll make sure Chloe is all set in our spare bedroom, Laura," Joy said. "I don't want you to worry about her. Tonight is about you and Adam reconnecting and I want you to have fun. I'll bring her back tomorrow around one o'clock. That will give me time to feed her and a window for you two to fit in one more sexy time."

"You're a saint, Joy," Laura said, grinning. "Both of you are. Thanks for taking care of my baby. Man, I hope I don't blow it. I might need to check for spiderwebs before he greases me up."

They all snickered. "You're going to be fine," Kayla said. After a round of quick hugs, and a kiss goodbye to Chloe, Laura watched them leave and resumed applying her makeup. The house was quiet, allowing her nerves to stew, and she took deep breaths to remind herself to stay calm.

Finally, the hour arrived. Laura gave her reflection one more glance. Her hair was silky and glossy, her makeup dark and sultry, her dress black and sexy. Hopefully, Adam would find her irresistible. Hearing the knock on the door, she slowly pulled it open and dramatically rested her arm on the frame.

"Hello, sailor," she said in her sultriest tone.

Adam's eyes widened, full of lust and desire as they swept over her body, and the nerves dissipated as if they'd never existed. Oh, yeah. He wanted her badly. Thrumming with anticipation, she urged him inside.

"Wow, Laura," he said, his Adam's apple bobbing as he swallowed. "You look amazing. I'm struggling to catch my breath here."

"Thank you," she said, noticing the flowers in his hand. "Are those for me?"

Nodding, he stepped forward, handing them to her. "They're carnations. The florist said they symbolize hope and love and motherhood. Since you've done such a great job with Chloe, I figured they were perfect. I'm so thankful for how you've raised her, Laura."

Tears burned her eyes as she took the flowers, inhaling the rich fragrance. "Thank you. I'm so grateful to you for forgiving me for...well, everything."

She laid the bouquet on the counter and he drew her to him, cupping her face. "There's nothing to forgive, sweetheart. Life happens. There's not a malicious bone in your body. You did your best and it's enough."

Lost in the sentiment in his sky-blue eyes, Laura slid her palms over his chest and cupped the back of his head. Pulling him to her, she enveloped his lips in a kiss of wonder, hope, and love. He kissed her back, his hand fisting in her hair, mussing it although she didn't give a damn. Aching to connect with him, she broke the kiss and stared into his eyes.

"Where did you make the reservation?"

"Atlantic Grill."

Her eyes darted between his. "Cancel it," she said softly.

His thumb swept over her cheek. "I want to earn you, Laura. You deserve that."

"You know what else I deserve?"

He grinned and shook his head.

"I deserve an extensive night of knocking boots. It's been so long, Adam. I don't want to wait anymore. Take me to bed. We can order food once you've been inside me. Please."

His pupils darted between hers as he contemplated. "How the hell am I supposed to say no to that?"

"You're not." Threading her fingers through his short hair, she commanded, "Fuck me, Adam. I need you."

Groaning, he pulled her into another searing kiss. His tongue warred with hers until she felt the familiar slickness between her thighs. Feeling the arousal build, she pressed her body against his, the buckle of his belt pushing against her stomach.

"Okay," he said, pulling back. His lips were swollen and wet, and she was taken by how handsome he was. With his angular features, stunning eyes and gorgeous smile, he was still the hottest man she'd ever seen. "Let me cancel the reservation. Damn, Laura. I wasn't expecting this." Pulling out his phone, he pulled up the app to cancel.

"I like keeping you on your toes, buddy. And there will be plenty of time for us to have dinner together. Might as well take advantage of the free babysitting."

Closing the app, he chuckled. "So true." Sliding his hands down her bare arms, he threaded his fingers through hers. "You look amazing tonight, Laura. It's stunning."

She breathed a laugh. "I actually spent time on my makeup. Figured you deserved more than 'tired mommy' if I wanted to rile you up."

"I'm always riled around you, kitten," he almost growled. "Don't you understand?  You're the sexiest woman I've ever been with.  I feel so incredibly lucky every time I touch your silky skin."

Her knees damn near buckled at the reverent words and he must've noticed because he crouched down and slid his arm behind them.  Lifting her, he carried her to the bedroom, gently laying her on the bed so her hair fanned across the pillow.

"Beautiful," he said, his gaze adoring as he stroked her hair.

"Take your clothes off," she demanded, lifting her arms above her head.  "I want to watch you undress for me."

He nipped her lips.  "Someone's bossy."

"You have no idea." Arching a brow, she said, "Off.  Now."

"Yes, ma'am."  Straightening, he began unbuttoning his dress shirt slowly, one clasp at a time.  "I think you're tougher than most of my drill sergeants."

Chuckling, she sank further into the bed, content to lounge and watch his magnificent body emerge from the clothing. "I'm pretty damn tough."

"You are," he said, tugging the shirt from his body and tossing it to the floor.  Eyes locked with hers, he slowly unbuckled his belt and unzipped his dress pants, lowering them to the floor and kicking off his shoes and socks.  Left in his boxer briefs, he panted as he stared down at her.

"The underwear too, soldier."

His lips formed an adorable pout.  "I want to see you too."

"Not yet," she said, biting her lip.  "This is too good."  Her gaze roved over his six-pack and muscular body, admiring how fit and sensual it was.  "God, you're so fucking hot.  It's not fair.  It makes me dream of things I shouldn't."

The corner of his lips curved.  "I want you to dream of me. As often as possible.  It gives me hope."

Wetness clouded her eyes as she wondered what he hoped for. A future with her? A time when they'd finally settle into a life together and raise Chloe as true partners? Her tender heart silently yearned for those things and she reminded herself to stay in the moment. They were possible if she and Adam stayed the course, and the prospect filled her with such optimism.

"Let me show you what I dreamed of last night," she said, rubbing her finger over her wet lip, loving how his eyes flashed with desire. "Take off your underwear and I'll demonstrate it in person."

Hooking his fingers over the band, he slid the garment off his hips, his erection standing proud and ready from his body. Grasping it in his hand, he slowly jerked the base. "Is this what you want?" he asked, the gravel in his low-toned voice making every cell in her body quiver.

"Yes," she whispered, sitting up and crawling to the center of the bed. Balancing on all fours, she licked her lips, ensuring they glistened. "Come here."

His breathing was labored as he approached her, thick cock in his hand, the mushroomed head pulsing. Sliding the palm of his free hand over her hair, he gently fisted it in his fingers. Beckoning him with her gaze, she opened her lips, gasping when he touched the head of his shaft to them.

"Yeah, kitten," he said, rimming her lips with the head of his cock. "Do you want me to fuck that sexy mouth?"

In reply, she extended her tongue, swiping it over the head before licking the length of his shaft. He cursed, fingers tightening in her hair, and Laura saw the tiny bead of moisture appear on the straining head. Touching it with her tongue, she licked it clean, loving how strong yet sensitive he seemed before her. Opening her mouth wide, she invited him in.

Hissing through his teeth, he slid into her mouth, groaning with desire when she closed around him. Bringing his other hand to her head, he gripped her hair, the possessive gesture driving her wild. Flattening her tongue, she sucked him deep, rimming the underside with gentle pressure as her lips enclosed his flesh.

"Laura," he breathed, lust in his slitted eyes as his hips undulated into her mouth. Purring around him, she strived to make it so good that he would crave her during the nights and hours they were apart. Oh, how she'd come to need him during those times and she wanted nothing more than to show him she could please him. That she was the only woman he would ever need.

Hollowing her cheeks, she created more suction, grabbing the base of his shaft and tugging as her mouth maneuvered over the sensitive flesh. The jutting of his hips increased until he was fucking her in earnest, shoving his cock to the back of her throat and then retreating, speaking reverent words of encouragement as she loved him.

"Fuck, baby, your mouth is magic," he said, clenching his fingers in her hair. "Look at me." Laura lifted her gaze to his ice-blue eyes, full of desire. "Do you like having my cock stuffed in that pretty mouth, kitten?"

She nodded, thrilled her actions were responsible for the flush that covered his strong body. Wanting to give him an explosive orgasm, she increased the pace of her hand at the base as her lips slid back and forth over the tight skin.

"Come in my mouth," she said, only breaking from her ministrations to give the hushed command.

"Are you sure, baby?"

Nodding, she tugged and pulled the straining flesh until the veins threatened to pop. Staring up at him, she pled with her gaze.

Adam called her name, holding her head steady as he plunged his hips toward her in a maddening rhythm. Breaths heaved from his lungs, the sounds ripping through the room until he shattered. Thick spurts of his release jetted against her throat and Laura closed her eyes, milking the head as he came inside her. His large body quaked, the undulations of his hips erratic, as he emptied every last drop inside her wet mouth. Finally, when the tiny pulses ceased, she lifted her lids to stare up at him.

So many emotions swam in his eyes. Adoration. Desire. *Love?* Laura couldn't be sure, but there was something in the sparkling depths. Something deep and true and heart-wrenching. Clutching on to it, she popped free of his shaft and licked her lips. "Mmmm..." she said, grinning up at him. "You taste so good."

"Holy shit," he breathed, tracing the pad of his thumb across her lower lip. "I certainly didn't think we'd start the evening that way."

Laughing, she nuzzled into his hand. "We've got all night, soldier. I have a feeling that's only the beginning."

Taking pity on his quaking frame, she tugged him toward the bed. He collapsed in a heap as she stretched out beside him.

"Why are you still dressed?" he asked, eyes narrowed.

"Because I spent a lot of time picking out this dress. I need you to admire it before you rip it off."

Stretching out on his side, he ran his hand along the silky fabric, over her side and down to her hip. "You look fantastic, Laura. You always do."

Her nose wrinkled as she stared at him from the opposite pillow. "You see me way too often as a mom. It's so unsexy. I wish we'd dated before I had Chloe. I was so hot then."

"Honey, you're gorgeous all the time," he said, rolling to cover half her body with his.  Leaning on his elbow, he caressed her face.  "The way you are with Chloe, it's so attractive to me.  To know you're such a good mother and we created her together.  It's so fucking beautiful."

Tears prickled her eyes.  "It is pretty damn awesome."

His expression was pensive as he studied her.  "Was the birth difficult?  I know there's a pretty intense range of pain for these things.  Erika told me her epidural didn't work for Christina and it was extremely painful."

"I was really lucky," she said, remembering the day her life had changed forever.  "Kayla and Joy were there and I had a C-section due to my *advanced age*," she snickered, "so it was completely painless."

His finger traced her cheek.  "I wish I could've been there."

"Me too," she whispered, the words violently true.  "I thought about you the whole time, wondering where you were and hoping you were okay.  I wanted so badly to share the experience with you."

"I missed so much with Chloe, but I missed things with you too.  Supporting you while you were pregnant, being there when you gave birth, the first days after she came home.  I'm really bummed I missed that, Laura."

"I know," she said, feeling a tear slide down her cheek.  "Our circumstances were just fucking terrible.  What a cluster."

Lowering, he kissed the tear away, trailing his lips over her face until he came to her lips.  "We could still experience those things together."

Her heart slammed in her chest.  "Sure.  If you have a time machine, we can head back right now and you'll be good to go."

"Do you want another child, Laura?" he asked, his expression filled with tenderness.  "It's something I've been thinking about a lot lately. I look at Chloe and realize how much I missed. I want to experience that...maybe with you if we can figure this thing out."

"Adam," she whispered, both delighted and frightened by his words. "I'm forty-three. I've pretty much given up on having another child."

"It's not impossible by any means," he said, brushing a sweet kiss across her lips. "I know quite a few people who have had kids well into their mid-forties. I just don't want you to rule anything out, sweetheart."

"Don't we have so many other things to figure out first?"

"Yes," he said, his lips quirking. "A shit ton of other things. But aren't we mature enough to say what we want? I care about you, Laura...and maybe more that I haven't quite figured out yet. I've lived enough to know that a connection and an attraction like ours don't come along every day. I think it would be really stupid to squander it."

Sliding her arms around his neck, she gave him a glowing smile. "I care about you and maybe more too," she whispered, realizing how true the words were. She'd pined for Adam for years, and in her heart, she knew she most likely loved him. After how amazing he'd been with Chloe and forgiving her for her omission, Laura understood what a good man he was. She could spend her whole life searching and never find someone as perfect for her as Adam.

"I'm not trying to freak you out or push either of us into something we're not ready for," he said. "But we're in our forties and I'm trying to figure out the next chapter of my life. If we're on our way to building something together, I don't want to waste time building something separate. Does that make sense?"

"Perfect sense," she said, exhilarated he was contemplating making their arrangement more serious. "And I've always wanted those things, Adam.  I just never found the right person.  Maybe you'll end up being my person.  That would be pretty damn awesome."

He arched a brow, contorting his face into something so sexy.  "Keep giving me blow jobs like that and I'll be your person every second of the damn day. Jesus, Laura, you're a fucking sex goddess."

Throwing her head back, she sighed in relief.  "Thank god.  I wasn't sure if I still had it.  It's been a long time for me."

"Oh, you've still got it, kitten," he said, sliding over her and nuzzling her nose with his.  "In spades.  And now it's time I return the favor.  How the hell do I get this dress off?"

Laughing, she urged him to sit so she could stand and undo the zipper.  Dragging it off, she stood before him in her strapless bra and thong.  His gaze was adoring as it roved over her.  "Come here, honey," he said, reaching for her.

Throwing caution to the wind, she stepped forward and never looked back.

# Chapter 15

Adam took in every inch of Laura's body. It was familiar, yet different, and he was overcome with the knowledge that their child had been responsible for the changes in her body. It stoked a possessive fire him, knowing she'd carried a part of him inside her, and he ached to caress every dimple and hollow.

Tugging her close, he ran his hand over her abdomen, tracing his fingers over her C-Section scar. "I was afraid you would think it was ugly," she said, cupping his shoulders as he caressed the quivering muscles of her abdomen.

"Never," he said, leaning down to kiss the scar. Wanting to reassure her, he smothered her belly and hips with butterfly kisses. "Every part of you is gorgeous, baby, and every part is mine." Gazing up at her, he cupped her mound, causing her to gasp. "This is *mine*, Laura. Do you understand?" She gasped at the authoritative words and he felt his lips curve in a sensual grin.

"Take it off," he said, fingering the underwire of her bra. Slipping her hands behind her back, she unclasped the garment and it slid to the floor. "The panties too, honey." She complied, shimming them down her hips and kicking them aside.

"Sorry," he said, grinning. "I'm feeling dominant tonight. I want to take you hard and claim you so you'll never think of another man."

"Adam," she whispered, cupping his jaw. "I never think of any man but you."

Growling, he grasped her hips and lifted her to the bed, loving her high-pitched squeal. Looming over her, he enveloped her lips in a passionate kiss, licking the depths of her mouth, marking her with his saliva. Trailing his lips down her nape, he brushed them across her collarbone, kissing the creamy skin that ran above her breasts. Moving lower, he nudged kisses around her nipple, arousal churning in his frame as the dark bud pebbled.

"They're bigger," he murmured, blowing on the sensitive nubbin.

"They were huge when I was breastfeeding. Now, they're still a bit bigger than they used to be. It's annoying when I jog because I have to stuff them into a sports bra."

"Poor baby," he said, rimming her nipple with his lips as she writhed beneath him. "I'd be happy to massage them for you after your runs."

Chuckling, she ran her hand over his hair. "I bet you would, buddy."

Smiling into her color-flecked eyes, he extended his tongue, lapping at the tight nipple as he held her gaze. "*Fuck*," she whispered.

"Soon, honey," he said, sucking the bud into his mouth, loving how she gazed back at him, eyes glassy and full lips wide. "I'm going to fuck you so hard." He tugged her between his lips, using his tongue to flick the tip as he gave her pleasure.

Moving to her other breast, he lavished it with the same attention until she was purring beneath him. Needing to taste her sweet honey, he skimmed his lips down her stomach, over her navel and reverently kissed her scar again before lowering to his knees beside the bed. Drawing her forward, he situated her legs over his shoulders.

"Give me that sexy pussy, kitten," he murmured, mouth searching her folds to find her dripping center. Extending his tongue, he lapped her essence, the taste so sweet upon his lips as her body bowed on the bed.

"Good girl," he breathed, lifting his fingers to spread her quivering folds. Searching with his index finger, he found her engorged nub, almost hidden behind the flushed skin. Preparing her, he lathered her clit with his tongue, ensuring it was wet and ready. Placing his fingers over the nub, he began rubbing concentric circles as he trailed his tongue back to her wet opening. Desperate to be inside her, he slipped into her tight channel, fucking her with his mouth as he rubbed her clit.

"*Ohmygod*," she groaned, the words rushed together as she pushed her core into his face. Loving how responsive she was, he increased the pressure of his tongue and fingers, determined to give her a mind-blowing orgasm.

"Adam," she cried, hands grasping his head as her body shuddered atop the comforter. "I'm so close. God, it feels so good. Don't stop!"

*No fucking way, kitten.* The words flitted through his overheated brain as his jaw and hand worked her into a frenzy of quaking nerves. When her body was strained and he knew she was close, he groaned into her sweet body, urging her to come.

Screaming unintelligible words, her back arched upon the bed and she exploded against him, her honeyed cream flowing over his tongue and chin. Consumed by her, he let her float until her body relaxed on the bed, breathing labored.  Nuzzling her trembling core, he realized how special it was to be with her like this again, after all the years he'd dreamed of her while he was deployed.  He'd been so sure she'd find someone else before he returned, and was overjoyed they'd reconnected before it was too late.  *Mine*, his brain whispered.  Fuck yes.  She was his and he wouldn't be stupid enough to let her go again.

Reluctantly removing his face from her drenched center, he grabbed his pants, pulling out the wallet and removing a condom.  Sliding it on, he stood and crawled over her spent body, lithe as a cougar.  Looming over her, he stared into her voluminous eyes.

"Laura," he breathed, pushing her thigh open to seat himself between her legs.  Sliding his hand behind her knee, he lifted her leg, opening her fully to him.  Touching the head of his cock to her folds, he navigated to her core.

Lifting her hand, she palmed his cheek and spoke words that drove him mad with lust.  *"Don't hold back."*

Listening to his woman, he plunged into her, his now-recovered cock stiff as a fucking rock and ready for round two.  Clenching his teeth, he hammered her, holding her knee to her shoulder so he could have greater access.

"Is this what you want?" he growled, consumed with pleasure from her taut channel squeezing his shaft.  "You want me to fuck that tight pussy, kitten?"

"Yes," she warbled, breasts jiggling as her body moved upon the bed.  The sight was so erotic, and her straining tissues around his cock were so choking, he thought he might die from pleasure.  "God, Adam, it feels so good."

"I know, baby," he said, lowering to kiss her, tongue surging inside her mouth to mimic the pace of his cock.  "Who does this tight, sweet pussy belong to?"

"You," she moaned, clenching his shoulders. "Oh, god, you. Adam, I missed you so much."

The words broke his heart and pieced it back together again, all at the same time. Staring into her heavy-lidded eyes, he realized the truth. She was it for him. The one woman he wanted to spend the rest of his life with. It was overwhelmingly intense yet surprisingly practical. When you knew, you just knew.

"I missed you too, sweetheart." He increased the pace, fucking her so fiercely that the sounds of their slapping flesh echoed off the walls. "I'm so glad I found you again."

"Me too," she cried, head thrown back as she took everything he gave her. "Oh, god, right there. Fuck, Adam, I'm going to come again."

"Yeah, honey," he said, working like hell to hit the spot deep inside and stimulate her clit with the base of his shaft at the same time. "Come all over me. Fuck, you're so gorgeous."

Suddenly, her body froze...and then she shattered in his arms, causing something so primal to well in his chest. Wanting to mark her in some way, he pressed his lips to her neck, sucking the tender skin between his teeth as he pummeled her. The walls of her slick channel convulsed around him and he lost it, shooting every drop of emotion into her soft body while she surrounded him with her legs. He was wrapped up in every inch of her skin and wondered if this was what heaven felt like. Drawing the soft skin of her neck between his lips, he tasted her essence, knowing he was drowning in her.

Her body shuddered as a chuckle spilled from her throat. "Are you sucking me?" she asked, her voice throaty and sexy as she nuzzled his cheek.

"Yes," he murmured against her neck, kissing the tender skin. "You're the only sustenance I need. You taste so good."

They lay there, lazy and sated, while their sweat-soaked bodies cooled.  Laura trailed her fingers over his neck and upper back, the sensation so magnificent that it enhanced his lingering shivers.  His fingers clutched her hair, unable to let go as his shaft softened in her body.

"Need to remove the condom," he murmured, hating he had to leave her tight warmth.

"Can't move," she mumbled.

He grunted, clutching her close and allowing himself another minute of being wrapped up in her.  Sighing, he placed a few tender kisses on her jaw and lifted, popping himself free of her sated body.  Once the condom was disposed of, he stretched out next to her.  Facing her, their bodies aligned as he caressed the hair at her temple.

"Hey," she said, smiling as his gaze held hers.

"Hey."

"Sometimes I wondered if I blew our first time out of proportion.  I remembered it being so fucking good."

"And?" he asked, grinning.

"Better.  It's even better now.  Holy shit, Adam.  You rocked my world."

Thrilled that she was pleased, he stroked her hair.  "That was amazing, honey.  It's an honor to be with you like that."

"Damn it," she said, nostrils flaring.  "Don't make me cry, okay?  I'm an emotional wreck right now.  Why are you so damn sweet?"

Chuckling, he shook his head.  "Maybe I'm only sweet so you'll let me love your delectable body."

Her cute nose scrunched.  "Doubtful.  On another note, I'm starving.  Let's order something."

"Pizza?" he asked, shrugging.  "It seems to be our go-to after some mind-blowing orgasms if I remember correctly."

"Yes." Her eyes lit with pleasure. "Pizza. I can already taste it. Where's your phone?"

"On the floor with the rest of my clothes. Does this mean I have to move?"

"Yes, buddy, you still owe me dinner. I want extra pepperoni and mushrooms since I didn't get a fancy spread at one of Manhattan's finest restaurants."

"Hey, that was all you. I was willing to woo you."

Sitting up, she waved her hand. "Plenty of time for that. Let me find my phone. We're going to stuff our faces and then you're going to fuck me again. Got it?"

Shooting up to sit on the bed, he grabbed her and threw her over his shoulder. Striding to the kitchen he lowered her so she could grab her phone from her purse on the counter. "Got it, woman. I'm going to ensure you can't even walk tomorrow."

Chucking her eyebrows, she dialed the number and lifted the phone to her ear. "Challenge accepted." Naked, she beamed up at him as she ordered.

# *Chapter 16*

♥

They lounged on the couch, munching the succulent pizza as they recounted stories from the years they'd been apart. Adam told her about his mission, leaving out classified details, and pride swelled in her chest at how brave he was. As he told her stories of raids and surges, he absently rubbed her legs as they stretched out over his. It was intimate and comfortable, and Laura knew she was toast. Yep, one night of great sex and she was head over heels.

Letting the love wash over her, it encompassed her as she pushed the fear away. This was Adam. Strong, honorable, sexy-as-hell Adam. Laura was pretty sure she'd never truly been in love before and if she had to fall for someone, she was so glad it was him. The father of her beloved Chloe and the man she wanted to build a future with.

She was still shocked that he'd brought up having another child as they lay together earlier. It was a serious subject and, in her experience, men were pretty terrible at serious. But Adam wasn't like the immature dolts she'd dated years ago as she'd navigated the scene in Manhattan. No, Adam was a *man*—mature and thoughtful and practical. It was so refreshing to meet an adult in their modern world and she realized it was one more reason to clutch onto him and never let go.

"The last piece is yours," he said, pointing to the box that lay open on the coffee table.

Reaching over, she picked it up and bit off the tip. She'd thrown on her robe and he wore his boxers, and the scene achingly reminiscent of their night together four years ago. "Guess you've realized the path to getting in my knickers is through pizza."

Laughing, he continued to trail his palm over her calf, the caress so gentle and almost possessive. "If that's all it takes, I'm a lucky man."

"It doesn't hurt that you're a pretty kick-ass dad. Chloe loves you, you know."

"Yeah?" he asked, excitement flashing in his eyes. "I really hope so. I sense that she enjoys our time together."

"She won't shut up about you. I'd be annoyed if it weren't so cute," she teased. *"Adam took me to the park. Adam is really good at puzzles. Adam's favorite color is blue too."* Her high-pitched tone mimicked Chloe's. "Geez, I get it. You're awesome. She's besotted by you."

His expression turned pensive. "I want to tell her I'm her dad, Laura."

Chewing the pizza, she regarded him. "Okay," she said, nodding. "Let's take her to the playground tomorrow together. We'll explain it to her then."

"Thank you," he said, his voice gruff with emotion. "I love her so much."

"I know," she said, throat thick as she swallowed. *It's why I love you so much.* Laura didn't say the words but they were true. Wrapped in the joy of loving a man with her entire soul, she let the feeling permeate her bones. After dinner, she lost herself to his skillful lovemaking until she fell asleep in his arms, clutching on for dear life.

The next afternoon they took Chloe to the park. Adam held Laura's hand as they walked, letting Chloe run ahead to hop on the merry go round.

"You seem to be walking okay today, sweetheart," he murmured into her ear. "I need to fuck you harder tonight."

Giggling, she shot him a look. "I'm sore as hell but it was so worth it. I haven't had a night like that...well, ever, really. I had no idea you could have that many orgasms in one night. You've created a monster. I want more."

Chuckling, he led her to the bench and they sat, watching Chloe as she played with one of the other kids nearby. "You can have it every night if we move in together, honey."

Her heart leaped into her throat and she felt her eyes grow wide. Grinning, he squeezed her hand. "Did I shock you? Sorry. I just think about it a lot."

Swallowing thickly, she asked, "Do *you* want to move in together?"

He shrugged, looking toward the blue sky as he contemplated. "It would give me so much more time with Chloe, and with you." He bumped his shoulder into hers. "I don't really see a downside."

Searching his clear eyes, she pondered. "Are we ready for that? I don't want to move too fast."

"Like I said last night, honey, I'm forty-two. I mean, you'll always be an old lady compared to me but I don't want to waste time when I know what I want."

She punched his arm at his teasing words. "I don't look a day over forty-one," she joked.

Laughing, he kissed her hand. "Eh, you're not ancient yet."

"I hate you," she said, scrunching her features.

"Look," he said, stretching his arm across her shoulders. "I'm in this, Laura. I don't want to be with anyone but you. I want to build my life around you and Chloe. I keep telling myself not to push too hard, but I'm someone who kind of bulldozes my way through life. I've always been this way. I think it drives my brother insane. When I feel something, I just feel it." Tucking a tendril of hair behind her hair, his lips curved. "I felt it that night when I saw you leaning over the balcony, looking like a mermaid who'd escaped the ocean. I just beelined right to you and never looked back."

"Yeah, I was pissed when you first walked up. You ruined my alone time."

His lips formed a cute pout. "Ouch."

"But you made up for it, don't worry. I was pretty happy with the intrusion once I saw how hot you were."

"Damn straight," he said, kissing her temple. "You were mad for me, woman."

Smiling, they lapsed into silence, watching Chloe play with the others as she laughed and twirled. Eventually, she ran up to them, holding a dandelion in her hand. Crouching down, Laura helped her blow the seeds so they trailed across the park.

"Adam, will you push me on the swing?" Chloe asked.

"In a minute, baby," Laura said before he could answer. Grasping her daughter's tiny arms, she smiled as her heart pounded in her chest. "Remember how we always talk about how George has the same eyes as Uncle Sam?"

Chloe nodded.

"Well, I'm not sure if you've noticed but you and Adam have the same eyes. When I look at both of you, I see the same exact color." Chloe looked at Adam, studying him. "Do you know why that is, honey?"

Chloe turned back to face her, shaking her head. "It's because Adam is your daddy just like Uncle Sam is George's daddy. When mommies and daddies have babies, their babies usually have either their mommy's or daddy's eyes."

Her tiny blue eyes widened as she lifted her gaze to Adam again. Laura could see the wheels churning in her brain as she contemplated.

"Adam is your daddy honey. He and I have been friends for a long time and we made you together. That's why you both have such pretty blue eyes."

Adam crouched down beside them and she could see tears shimmering in his glassy orbs. "I'm so proud to be your dad, Chloe. I love you very much."

Chloe broke into a huge smile and lifted her arms to Adam. "I love *you!*" she exclaimed, placing a kiss on his lips when he enveloped her in a hug. His gaze lifted to Laura's as he held their daughter, tears streaming down his handsome face. *Thank you*, he mouthed, and she nodded, fighting her own tears. They were a unit now, stronger together than they'd ever been apart. Adam reached for her hand and she held it tight, realizing her life would never be the same. Standing, they wiped their tears and each held Chloe's hand as they trailed to the swings, promising to push her high as they exchanged looks filled with love.

That night, they both read to Chloe and tucked her in, the weight of their earlier revelation to her between them. Once she was fast asleep, Laura pulled him to her room, needing so badly to hold him.

"Stay with me tonight," she whispered, pulling him into a kiss. "I need you, Adam."

His expression was unreadable. "Are you okay that I'll be here when she wakes up?"

Nodding, Laura tugged him to the bed. "Yes. Make love to me."

In between kisses, they discarded their clothes. When they were naked, Adam sheathed himself and joined her in bed. Laura climbed over him, lifting his shaft and aligning the head with her entrance. Lowering herself onto him, she balanced on her palms beside his head on the pillow, moving herself up and down his length as he cupped her breasts. His skilled fingers tweaked her nipples, driving her wild as she rode him. Striving to ensure they came together, she found the right angle, rubbing her clit over his shaft as he pushed into her, over and over.

"I saw you like this," he rasped, his hands roving over her body. "So many nights. So many dreams."

Lowering her lips to his, she sucked away the words, eradicating the past. Living without him had been heartbreaking and so very lonely. Grateful that he was here, Laura never wanted to visit the past again. There was only the future, *their* future, together. Lost to passion, they strained against each other until their bodies exploded. Adam's strong arms surrounded her, drawing her into his chest as they struggled to regain the ability to breathe. Rubbing her lips on his neck, she asked, "Your place or mine?"

"Huh?" he grunted, still lost in the haze of his desire.

"If we move in together. Your place or mine?"

She could almost feel his smile as his arms tightened around her. "Yours. It's a three-bedroom because you're rich as shit. I've got a one-bedroom rental. Sorry I can't afford more. I can pay you in orgasms."

Snickering, she nodded against his skin. "Deal."

There, in the aftermath of their heated coupling, they fortified their decision to take the next step in their burgeoning relationship.

## *Chapter 17*

♥

The newly cemented family unit fell into step, Adam spending most of his nights at Laura's house. After speaking with his landlord, he confirmed he'd be able to sublet his apartment for the rest of the lease term so he could make the full-time move to Laura's home. Fall was setting in, with winter close behind, and Adam wanted to have everything moved before it turned too cold.

Although he was excellent with money and had a robust savings and financial portfolio, he was nowhere near as well-off as Laura. Wealth like hers mostly existed from family inheritances and he always pushed away the nagging fear that he was an interloper. Whenever he brought up their finances, she would wave him off and tell him she didn't give a damn. He'd set up the child support accounts for Chloe months ago when they'd reconnected and contributing to those brought him solace. Usually, when his thoughts drifted to the morose subject, his sexy woman would tell him to stop worrying and seduce away his fears. At least he could give her pleasure and he was so thankful for their endless chemistry. Never had he been so attracted to someone. Their fiery couplings were everything he'd ever imagined.

One afternoon, as he hung with Carter and Sam, watching the kids at Sam's apartment while the ladies got pedicures, he took a swig of his beer as he contemplated them. "Have either of you guys met Laura's mom?"

"Not me," Sam said, "but Carter met her years ago."

Carter shot him a sardonic glare. "She came to one of my plays and told me she was offended because my character said the 'F' word three times."

"Yikes. Is she really stuffy like that?"

"Yeah, from what I remember," Carter said, nodding. "She's kind of a salty old broad. I can actually see where Laura gets it from. But Laura is kind and compassionate, where her mother seemed cold and snobby. Kayla says Laura doesn't spend a lot of time with her, especially since the falling out when she got pregnant."

Adam's eyebrows drew together. "They had a falling out?"

"Dude, her mom was pissed that she was knocked up from a one-night stand. Threatened to find a way to ensure her trust wouldn't go to her unless she got an abortion. Laura told her to shove it and Kayla promised to throw the full weight of the law into protecting her inheritance. Eventually, the old bat calmed down and Laura got her trust. But it was pretty intense there for a while."

"Wow," Adam said, blowing a breath through puffed cheeks. "I had no idea."

"I think Laura's let it go," Sam said, "but it's important you know how much she was willing to give up to have Chloe, Adam. She wanted her with her whole heart."

"That's pretty damn amazing," Adam said, sinking into the couch as he contemplated. "Just one more reason to love her. I've never met anyone like her."

"No way," Carter said, grinning. "Are you guys at the L-word phase? Congrats, man."

Adam saluted him with his beer. "We haven't technically said it out loud but it's definitely true for me, and I think it is for her. She's the one, guys. I love her so damn much. I want to have another kid with her."

"Hot damn," Carter said, rising to give Adam a fist bump before heading to the kitchen to grab another beer. "That's awesome. Kayla and I decided to stop after the twins because both our careers are insane, but she'll be thrilled to help Laura along the way."

"So will Joy," Sam said, beaming. "We all will. Congrats, brother."

"Well, I need to accomplish a few things first," Adam said, shrugging. "I need to tell her I love her, convince her to marry me, propose, tie the knot and *then* hopefully get pregnant. But we're on our way."

"Take it from us two schmucks who are desperately in love with our women, marriage is a wild ride but it's awesome with the right person. And that's me saying that. It's a freaking miracle." The three of them clinked their beers, enjoying the camaraderie of the lazy afternoon until their ladies returned and enveloped them in blazing embraces.

L aura was prepping for bed when Adam approached and kissed her shoulder in the reflection. Smiling, she brushed a kiss across his temple. "What was that for?"

Resting his chin on her shoulder, he gave her a reverent smile. "The guys told me about your mom and what a jerk she was to you when you were pregnant. I'm so sorry, Laura. I wish I'd been here to help you handle that."

"No one can handle my mother when she decides to go on a rampage. Believe me. You were safer with the Taliban."

"Wow. That bad, huh?"

"That bad," she said with a nod.

After a moment, he said, "I want to meet her."

Laura's gaze locked with his. "No."

"Laura, you're the woman I want to spend the rest of my life with. I have to meet her eventually. Come on."

Turning, she laid her palms over his pecs. "Not to be a dick, but you're the man who knocked me up and left me after a one-night stand. I know our story has way more nuance than that, but that's how she sees it. She'll decimate you. I won't set you up for that."

"Sweetheart, I've dealt with terrorists and rebel faction warriors. I think I can handle your mother."

"Don't count on it," she mumbled.

"I'm firm on this, honey. I want to meet her. Let's just rip the band-aid off and do it."

Sighing, Laura shook her head, staring at the bathroom counter as she contemplated. "Fine," she said eventually. "I'll set up brunch but don't say I didn't warn you. She's going to try and make you feel like the smallest bug on the bottom of her shoe. She's cowered some of the most powerful men in Manhattan. You'd better bring your A-game."

"I will," he said, brushing her lips with his. "And no one treats my woman like crap. I've got you, Laura. You'll always be protected with me."

Knowing the words were true, Laura let her sexy man carry her to bed and show her how protective and possessive he could truly be.

# Chapter 18

On Sunday, Adam placed a supportive hand on Laura's lower back as they entered the restaurant. He could tell she was dreading brunch with her mother and almost felt bad for pushing her into it. But he wanted to get to know the woman who'd raised Laura, and who'd treated her so badly during her pregnancy. Since he hadn't been there for Laura in the past, he felt an urge to take responsibility and explain his actions. Their circumstances were a product of an explosive connection and terrible timing.

The hostess led them to the table and a white-haired woman with austere features stood, extending her hand to Adam. "Hello," she said, her voice gruff. "You must be the man who placed his hands on my unmarried daughter and left her with an unwanted child. Miriam Cunningham." Lightly grasping his hand, she shook it.

Laura rolled her eyes. "Seriously, Mother? We haven't even sat down yet. Could you hold the judgmental statements until I get a mimosa?"

"It's a pleasure to meet you, Mrs. Cunningham," Adam said, releasing her hand and refusing to rise to the bait. Laura had prepared him for her chilly attitude and he was ready. They ordered brunch and mimosas, Miriam sticking to sparkling water and hot tea because alcohol made one's skin wrinkle.

"Guess I'm going to be a wrinkled old hag," Laura mumbled, sipping the orange liquid.

"I was disappointed you didn't bring Chloe today, Laura. You know I like to see her when I can."

"Yes," Laura said, nostrils flaring. "She always comes in handy when you need a sympathetic figure at one of your fundraisers or events. We have no place for those things in our life, Mother. I'm raising Chloe to be a child who accepts everyone, no matter how rich or poor they are. I think it's better we stick to major holidays as we've agreed upon. You get to spend one-on-one time with her, which I think does you both good."

"Well, I'm happy to know you're a parenting expert," Miriam grumbled, stirring her tea.

"More so than you," Laura quipped.

Adam squeezed her leg above the knee and she shot him a glare of death. Wanting to make peace, he tried to venture into polite conversation. "So, Mrs. Cunningham, Laura tells me you've lived in the Upper East Side neighborhood since you were young. I'd love to hear your favorite places. I'm new to the city and am still getting to know the nuances."

Miriam's resulting glare was cold but resigned. "Yes, let's discuss my home. A much safer topic. Well, if you want to see some fantastic art and collectibles, The Frick Collection at the Gilded Age mansion is lovely..." She trailed off into a detailed recounting of her most frequented spots in the neighborhood. It was a nice reprieve, allowing them to have a pleasant brunch until the bill came. Adam reached for it but Miriam swiped it before he could.

"I will take care of this," she said, putting on her glasses and looking over the check. "Laura tells me you don't have a paying job at the moment and that your savings are meager at best. I don't get to see her often and am happy to pay."

Hurt sliced through him as Laura glowered at her mother. He could almost envision puffs of steam exiting her ears as she stewed. Had she actually said that about him to her mom? He was already sensitive about how financially inequal they were. Did she look down on him for being middle class?

They paid the bill and walked onto the sidewalk, Laura giving her mother a frosty hug before Miriam nodded goodbye to him. Sliding into the black town car as the driver held the door open, she gave a brief wave before they drove away.

"For the love of god," Laura said through clenched teeth, hands fisted at her sides. "She's so damn infuriating. I'm so sorry, Adam. Don't listen to anything she said. She likes to twist things."

Struggling with the sting from Miriam's words, he nodded.

"I mean it," she said, sliding her palms over his cheeks. "You're amazing and you have everything Chloe and I ever need. Are we clear?"

"Yes," he said, sliding his arm around her waist and placing a soft kiss on her lips. "I just want to be able to give you what you deserve, sweetheart."

"You already do," she said, her smile so genuine. "This is why I didn't want you to meet her. She's toxic. Please let it go. Now that you've met, I can go back to my standard holiday schedule with her. Believe me, it's all I can take."

"She's definitely a pill," he said, determined to push the fears away. In his arms, he held a stunning, loving woman who stared up at him as if he were a damn hero. That was all he needed. It was enough.

"She's an irritable old bat. It got worse after Father died, although he was kind of stuffy too."

"How in the hell did you turn out so normal?"

Scoffing, she slid her hands around his neck. "The fact that you think I'm normal means my mission has been accomplished. I'm nothing of the sort, my friend."

He brushed a tendril of hair from her face. "You're perfect, Laura. Sexy, funny, caring. It's amazing considering your proximity to the woman I just met."

"Speaking of sexy," she said, arching a brow. "Kayla is watching Chloe until five o'clock. That gives us exactly," she looked at her phone, noting the time, "two hours and twenty-three minutes of sexy times. Take me home and ravish me before our little monster comes back."

"Honey," he said, pulling his phone from his pocket. "I'll have an Uber here in three minutes flat." Enamored by her resulting smile, he summoned the car as fast as his fingers would let him.

<h1 style="text-align:center">Chapter 19</h1>

A s the days grew colder, Adam set about packing his apartment. His subletter was moving in December first and he wanted to have everything moved to Laura's home before then. Due to his various deployments, he didn't have a ton of furniture or possessions, so moving would be relatively easy.

One day in mid-November, his brother came over to help him pack. Although Aaron had now met Laura several times, most often when they'd shared playdates with Christina and Harry, his brother was still distrustful of the informal custody agreement. As Aaron slipped on his jacket after they'd packed up Adam's small office, he pulled out a manilla envelope and laid it on the small table by Adam's front door.

"I drew up formal custody papers for you," Aaron said, holding up his hands when Adam opened his mouth to argue. "I don't want to fight with you. It just makes me extremely uncomfortable, Adam. At least look them over so I can tell myself you did it. Then, if you don't want to sign them, throw them away."

"I'm moving in with her, Aaron. I plan on proposing to her over the next few months and hopefully having another child. I have no intention of taking her to court."

"Marrying her won't give you custody of Chloe, Adam. You still have to formally petition the courts for that."

"We've discussed it and once we're married I'm going to formally adopt Chloe. I'm getting pretty pissed that you don't trust her, Aaron. I'm going to spend the rest of my life with her. I need you to get on board."

His brother sighed and shook his head. "Being a family lawyer is demoralizing, bro. I've seen so many happy couples devolve into nasty divorces and terrible custody battles. I guess I'm just wary. Look, I'm happy you love her. From the times I've met her, she seems pretty awesome. But even great people can have disastrous relationships. That's all I'm saying. Think about it. See you on Sunday." Pivoting, he exited the apartment, Adam's jaw clenching at his insistence on discussing the subject.

Pulling the papers from the envelope, he read them over, hating how formal they looked. Throwing them back on the table, he dismissed them. He'd toss them out when garbage day came. Checking his phone, he realized it was time to meet Laura and Chloe at McDonald's. They'd chosen the one near his apartment so he could maximize packing time and he headed out into the chilly day to meet them.

As he was walking, the hairs on the back of his neck stood to attention. A woman stepped onto the sidewalk and gently grasped his arm.

"Can I help you?"

Removing her scarf and glasses, Adam realized it was Miriam. "Hello, young man. Laura told me you were meeting her at the fast-food restaurant today." The way her nose turned up at *fast-food* reinforced her snobbery. "Laura has informed me of your intention to move in with her."

Adam studied her, wondering if he should ask the woman's permission to marry Laura. It was customary to ask a parent's permission in the South, but the rules were a bit more relaxed in New York and Laura sure as hell didn't seek her mother's approval to do anything.

"She's only keeping you close to rankle me," she said, scowling. "Laura has a wild spirit and will do anything to spite me that she can."

"I love her, Mrs. Cunningham, and I love Chloe. We want to make a life together and I'm sorry if you're not on board with that."

She scoffed. "And what kind of life can you give her? A poor vagabond who spent years in the desert while she raised your child on her own. You're a disgrace. Although I don't see eye to eye with Laura on many things, she's a Cunningham and deserves a man worthy of her."

"Look, lady," he said, feeling the anger simmer. "You've got a lot of nerve telling me I'm worthless. I've fought for years so ungrateful people like you can remain free and safe. That's worth more than some stupid trust fund your grandparent's parents passed down. I can see why Laura stays the hell away from you. You're a sad, pathetic old woman. I'd suggest you leave us alone if you want to continue seeing Chloe on holidays. You're already on thin ice." Dismissing her, he began to walk away.

"Wait," she said, grabbing his arm. Reaching in her pocket, she pulled out a white envelope. "Here, take it. I'm offering it to you in exchange for leaving Laura and never having contact with her again. There is a family friend whose son has agreed to marry her, even with her illegitimate child. Laura and Thurston dated after she had Chloe and he's always carried a torch for her. If you let her go, I firmly believe she will marry him. He will be able to offer Chloe a much better life than you can. Goodbye, Adam. I hope this is the last time we speak. Take the money and build something for yourself away from my daughter." With a tilt of her head, she replaced her glasses and scarf and shuffled down the street.

Adam's hands shook with fury as he opened the envelope. Inside was a check made out to him in the amount of a million dollars. Unable to believe the bizarre confrontation, his eyes bugged at the staggering amount. How much must Miriam hate him to spend that much to extricate him from Laura's life? And who the hell was Thurston? Laura had assured him she hadn't dated anyone while he was deployed. Frustrated and furious, he stuffed the check back in the envelope and into his jacket pocket, determined to let the anger go before he even considered telling Laura about the confrontation...or asking her about the mysterious Thurston...

# Chapter 20

Laura sat beside Adam on the bench as the kids played under the bright November sky. It was almost Thanksgiving and Laura was already dreading the annual holiday meal with her mother. She'd spent countless minutes on the phone with her mother discussing the menu and internally figuring out how many hours she could tolerate with her. Maybe they could get out of it and just attend Christmas dinner this year. Eyeing Adam, she postulated that he wouldn't give a damn since he seemed to have a distaste for her mother too. Laura felt it was important that Chloe get to know Miriam in small snippets—after all, family was family—but she was determined to keep the encounters infrequent so her mother's temperamental nature wouldn't taint her baby. Chloe was precious and sweet and loving and there was no way Laura would let Miriam's general nastiness and latent moroseness rub off on her.

Studying Adam, she noticed his tense shoulders and pensive expression. Something had been off with him ever since they'd had lunch at McDonald's last week. He was close to having all of his things moved to Laura's place. Was he having second thoughts? Did he think they'd moved too quickly? They'd been discussing marriage, Chloe's adoption and even having a second child, but the conversations were broad and they hadn't cemented any details. Perhaps he thought they were too heavy to be having before he moved in. Maybe he just wasn't ready for that level of commitment yet. She'd judged him ready and willing to move forward with a permanent, serious relationship but she'd been wrong before.

"You okay there, buddy?" she asked, nudging him with her shoulder. "You've been quiet lately."

"Yeah," he said, relaxing back and placing his arm across her shoulders. He felt so strong and sure, and she sunk into his warmth. "I've just got a lot on my mind."

Laura licked her lips, suddenly nervous. "We've moved pretty fast, Adam. I understand if you're freaking out. Taking on a partner and kid is a lot to deal with. Maybe you're longing for your single days."

His lips twitched. "Nope. I told you, Laura, I'm in this." His hand squeezed her shoulder. "And how about you? Do you ever miss dating or still think of anyone else from your past?"

It was such a strange question that her features scrunched together. "Um, yeah...I thought I told you. There hasn't been anyone since you. My lady parts were put out to pasture until you resurrected them. Thank goodness you came along."

He nodded, seeming unsure of her words, and a pit of unrest settled in her stomach. There was something he wasn't telling her and it frightened her. After everything in their past, they needed to be open and honest if their relationship was going to work.

"Adam," she said, turning her body toward his. "I can tell something's wrong. What is it? Talk to me."

A muscle ticked in his jaw and she realized he was pissed. Wracking her brain, she searched for what she could've done to anger him. Suddenly, a high-pitch scream wailed from the playground and they both jumped to attention. Christina and Chloe were crying as they lay on the ground, blood gushing from their foreheads.

"They were racing and both got caught up in the merry-go-round," Aaron said as they rushed to the crying children. "We need to call an ambulance now."

Laura pulled Chloe into her arms, overcome with terror as blood gushed out of her forehead. "Here, baby," she said, pulling tissues from her bag and holding them against the large gash. She handed some to Adam to give to Aaron to do the same for Christina. Adam called 911 and assured them the ambulances would be there in two minutes.

"I want Daddy to hold me," Chloe cried, reaching for Adam.

Laura's heart swelled in her chest as Adam reached for her. It was the first time she'd called him that and tears welled in his eyes as he clutched her against his chest. "There are some bandages and gauze in my medicine cabinet," he said, handing his keys to Laura. "Want to run and get them?"

Nodding, Laura grabbed the keys and sprang into action. Adam's apartment was only half a block away and she sprinted there, flung open the front door and ran to the bathroom, frantically raiding the medicine cabinet. Once she had the supplies, she trailed back to the front door and noticed something from the corner of her eye.

Glancing down, she saw a stack of formalized papers that read *"In the Matter of a Proceeding for Custody, Family Court of the State of New York, County of Manhattan."* Laura's heart leaped into her throat. Was Adam contemplating suing her for custody? He'd been so agreeable to proceeding without court intervention. Picking up the envelope on top of the petition, she opened it. Inside was a check...from her mother...for a million dollars. Reeling, she collapsed against the wall, unable to breathe. Had her mother attempted to pay Adam off? Was he considering taking the money and filing for custody?

Unable to reconcile the thoughts, especially while her baby was hurt on the playground, she decided she'd digest the shock later. Placing the check back in the envelope, she gathered the supplies that had fallen to the ground, locked Adam's apartment behind her and jogged back to the playground. Grilling Adam could wait—and oh, how she would grill him. To say she was stunned and dismayed would be an understatement. For now, she rushed to her little girl and applied the gauze to her forehead as Adam and Aaron worked alongside her.

Hours later, they were exhausted when they entered Laura's apartment, Chloe almost asleep in Adam's arms. They prepped her for bed and sat by her side until she'd fallen asleep, a large bandage covering the six stitches she'd needed on her forehead. Closing her door softly behind them, Laura trailed to the kitchen, Adam behind her. Crossing her arms, she leaned on the counter.

"That was intense," he said, crossing his arms and resting on his hip as well. "Man, Laura, I was terrified."

She nodded. "It happens when you have a kid. Each time she so much as stubs her toe I think I'm going to lose it. I just don't want her to experience any pain."

"I get it," he said, running his hand over his hair.

Silence stretched between them, uncomfortable and thick.

"So, we're both straight shooters, Adam, and I think it's time we hashed some stuff out."

"Okay," he said, expression unreadable.

"You've been distant lately.  What gives?  Did I do something to piss you off?"

Sighing, he shook his head.  "No.  There's just been a lot going on."

Her eyebrows lifted.  "I'm sure.  What with you having clandestine meetings with my mother to pick up payoff checks and drawing up custody papers, you've most likely been very busy."

Narrowing his eyes, he scowled.  "You saw them when you went to my apartment today."

It wasn't a denial, and that ripped Laura to shreds.  Feeling her world start to crumble, she was hit with the realization that he'd been plotting behind her back.  "Yes.  So, I guess that's it.  We keep secrets from each other now."

"*You're* lecturing *me* on keeping secrets?" he asked, his tone angry.

"You son of a bitch," she hissed, wanting to keep their voices low so they wouldn't wake Chloe.  "You're never going to truly let it go, are you?  I'm sorry I kept her from you for so long.  It was wrong and I've beat myself up for it so many times, I don't know what to do anymore.  I can't keep apologizing, Adam.  You need to accept my apology or move on."

A muscle ticked in his jaw.  "Who is Thurston?  Did you date him when I was deployed?  Because your mother seems to think I'm in the way of you marrying the love of your life who isn't a poor, hapless soldier."

A humorless laugh escaped her lips.  "My mother would say anything to manipulate my life to what she deems best.  I thought you understood that.  I'm certainly not going to stand here and let you accuse me of something that isn't true."

"And yet you're so sure I'm plotting against you to take Chloe and secretly meeting with your mom. Pretty hypocritical, Laura."

Sighing, she placed her forehead in her hand, rubbing harshly. "You need to leave before I say something I can't take back. When I get scrappy, it gets ugly, Adam. I need some time to digest this."

"Fine," he said, breezing past her. "Call me when you're willing to speak to the man who isn't good enough to shine your shoes. I'll be ready when *your highness* has time." Tears welled in her eyes as she watched him give a regal, mocking bow by the door. Then, he yanked it open and stalked away, anger vibrating from his strong frame.

Locking the door behind him, Laura buried her face in her hands, collapsed to the floor and allowed the tears to fall.

# Chapter 21

Two days later, Laura stood on her rooftop, arms balanced on the balcony as Kayla and Joy flanked her. Silent, they stared out over the bustling city.

"I'm loving this warm front," Kayla said, eyes closed as she inhaled the Manhattan air. "It's gorgeous for late November."

Laura nodded. "Chloe and I spent some extra time at the park yesterday soaking up the rays. I also did my best to prep her for this week's Thanksgiving lunch with Miriam the Marauder."

Joy snickered. "I'd love to see her face if she knew what you called her behind her back."

"Who says it's always behind her back?" Laura murmured.

Checking her phone, Kayla gave Laura a tender smile. "Carter and Sam will be back from the park with the kids soon. What are you going to do about Adam, Laura? You need to figure this out, especially with the holidays approaching."

"I know," she said, running her palms over the bumpy concrete surface. "I need to sit down and talk to him. I was just so fucking mad. He had formal custody papers drawn up, guys. If he tries to take my baby away, I'll decimate him. It's not happening."

"I remember a time not so long ago when you were the one who owed Adam an explanation," Joy said, gazing up at her. "You asked him to be understanding and hear you out and he was wonderful about everything. You owe him the same."

Laura wrinkled her nose. "You know, it's really annoying that you're right about everything, Joy. Could you maybe join us mortals and make a mistake or two sometime?"

Snickering, Joy shook her head. "Nope. I love being perfect."

Kayla snorted. "Um, okay."

The three of them contemplated in silence until Laura spoke. "I'm going to call him and schedule a time when we can talk. If one of you could watch Chloe when we meet, that would be awesome."

"You've got it, sister," Kayla said. "We really want you guys to work this out. Adam completes our friend family, Laura. We love him and he's Chloe's father. You love him too, even though you haven't said it out loud for some unfathomable reason. You need to buck up and marry him. It's time."

Laura smiled. "That's pretty much the exact speech I gave Carter about you."

"Well, it worked. Hopefully, my speech will be just as effective. Adam's a remarkable man and an exceptional father, Laura. Plus, he's hot as hell and amazing in bed. I honestly don't understand why you're not there now, begging him to come back."

Laura chewed her lip. "I love him, guys. I think I always have, ever since the first night we met. It makes absolutely no sense but it's always been there."

Joy sighed. "So romantic."

Pulling her phone from her pocket, Laura dialed Adam's number. He answered on the third ring.

"Hello?"

"Hey," she said, sparing glances at Kayla and Joy. "I'm here with the ladies and they're telling me I'm being a complete asshole. They're probably at least eighty percent correct."

He was quiet for a moment and said, "Only eighty percent?"

Chuckling, she grinned. "Maybe more. I won't know until we sit down and compute it. I need to see you."

"Okay. I can be at your place in half an hour."

Holding her hand over the phone, she asked, "Can one of you watch Chloe for a few hours?"

"Yes!" they said in unison.

"All right. Chloe's going to hang with the ladies while we chat. Come on over anytime."

"See you soon, kitten."

The words sent a rush of desire and hope through her nervous frame. "See you soon."

# Chapter 22

♥

Adam arrived, looking contrite and sexy-as-hell as he stood on her doorstep. Motioning him in, she headed to the fridge and pulled out two beers. "Seems like we do best at awkward conversations when we're drinking one of these." Arching a brow, she handed him the bottle.

"That we do," he said, popping off the top and clinking it with hers. "To us." The low-toned words enveloped her and her heart began to thrum in her chest.

"To us," she said before taking a sip. Leading him to the couch, he sat beside her. "How many more difficult conversations do you think we're going to have on this couch?"

"I'd say none but I don't foresee that happening, Laura." His lips quirked into a smile. "I'm pretty stubborn and you're pretty headstrong, so there will probably be a lot more."

"Damn straight," she muttered, taking another sip before setting the bottle on the table. "I'll take headstrong any day over being a doormat. Okay, give it to me. The more I thought about it, there's no way you intentionally met with my mother. Did she seek you out?"

He nodded. "James Bond style—scarf, glasses and all. She wanted to save you from marrying a destitute wretch and informed me you'd be better off with Thurston.  What a stupid fucking name, by the way.  Sorry, but it's ridiculous."

Laura snickered. "It's completely absurd. Did she tell you I dated him?"

"Yep."

She rolled her eyes. "She wishes.  He's one of the douches she was always pushing in my path.  I did accompany him, my mother and his mother to a few brunches while I was pregnant.  I could only tolerate being in her presence if there were other people around because she was so awful when we were one-on-one.  I swear, Adam, we never dated.  He's not my type at all.  I find I like sexy, handsome soldiers much better."  She waggled her eyebrows.

"Thank god," he said, grasping her hand and rubbing it with his thumb.  "I never should've believed her and I'm sorry I did."  His gaze was genuine as he stroked her skin.  "It rankled me, Laura.  I'm already so sensitive about the fact that you have more money than I'll ever be able to make.  It makes me feel inadequate and that I'll never deserve you."

"Adam," she whispered, inching closer.  "Deserving someone isn't about how much money they have.  I don't give two craps about that.  I love you with all my heart.  I'd love you if you were broke on the street and lived in a box.  I mean, my apartment's much nicer, but you get my drift."

His Adam's apple bobbed before his lips curved into a euphoric grin.  "You finally said it out loud."

"Yeah," she said, giving an affable shrug.  "I should've said the words aloud before now.  I think I was scared.  I'm pretty sure I fell in love with you the night we met.  Remember when you were asking me what I told Chloe about her dad and there was something else I wanted to say?"

He nodded.

"I always told her that Mommy loved her dad very much. It was true, Adam. It always has been."

"Laura," he breathed, setting his bottle on the table. Dragging her across his lap to straddle him, he cupped her face. "I've waited so long to hear that from you. It means so much. You captured my heart the first night we met too. I pined for you for all those years. I was terrified you were going to think I was a stalker when I tracked you down at John's grave but I just didn't care. I needed to reconnect with the woman who'd consumed my soul."

Drawing her in for a poignant kiss, he said against her lips, "I love you so much, sweetheart. You're the one. My partner for the rest of my life. I can't do this without you."

Wrapping her arms around his neck, she consumed him in a blazing kiss, needing to show him how much she'd missed him...how much she'd come to depend on his calm patience and understanding demeanor. He balanced her completely and she was so thankful he'd had the courage to approach her by the sea all those years ago.

"So, you're not going to sue me for custody?" she teased, nipping his bottom lip.

He rolled his eyes. "My brother is an overprotective but well-meaning lawyer. He drew up the papers to protect me, even though I told him it was pointless. I was going to throw them out along with your mom's check. Although a million dollars would be nice." He glanced at the ceiling, pretending to ponder.

"Oh, no, buddy," she said, laughing down at him. "Not even a million dollars can get you out of this mess. You're stuck with me."

"Thank god," he growled, drawing her back in for a passionate kiss.

When she finally lifted her head, she slid her hand along his jaw. "I'm sorry. You're right that I'm headstrong. I actually kind of dig being that way. I'm tough and I'm a scrapper. I can't promise your life with me will be easy but I can certainly promise that it will be filled with lots of love and passion. If you'll have me."

"I want all of you, Laura. Every last frustrating, magnificent piece. I don't need easy. I just need you, honey."

Resting her forehead against his, she nuzzled his nose. "Chloe won't be home for two hours."

"Is that so?" he asked, running his hands over the globes of her ass as they strained from her tight jeans.

Laura nodded and yelped when he lifted her. Setting her on her feet, he led her to the side of the couch, turning her to face the arm. Reaching around, his front aligned with her back as he unbuttoned her jeans and slid the zipper down. Crouching down, he slid the jeans off her legs, urging her to step out of her shoes as well. Grasping the hem of her shirt, he pulled it over her head, tossing it to the floor. Trailing kisses over her shoulders, he unclasped her bra, leaving her naked before him.

Splaying his broad hand over her back, he gently urged her forward so she lay over the arm of the couch, ass thrust high in the air. Knowing she was fully exposed was thrilling and she glanced back at him as her face rested on the soft cushion.

"When were you last tested?" he asked, so sexy as he pulled his shirt over his head and began unbuttoning his pants.

"Six months ago. Everything was clean."

"Almost a year ago for me and I haven't been with anyone but you since then," he said, naked now as he approached her. Palming the mounds of her ass, she shivered as he caressed the sensitive globes. "I'm clean, honey, and I want to make love to you skin to skin.  I can pull out if you want or we can try and have another baby.  It's up to you."

It was something they'd discussed quite often and Laura realized she was ready.  She also knew that Adam wanted another child and she wanted so badly for him to enjoy the full experience she'd had with Chloe.  Swallowing thickly, she said, "Fuck me raw and come inside me.  I want it all, Adam.  I want everything with you."

"God, I love you," he said, spreading her ass apart with his firm hands.  Sliding his middle finger between the twin mounds, he glided it between her sensitive folds. Encircling her opening, he hissed.  "You're already wet."

"I always am around you.  You're hot as hell, soldier."

He shot a sexy smile over her shoulder.  Eyes cemented to hers, he nudged his finger inside her wet channel.  "I can't wait to feel your wet pussy around my cock, baby."

Laura mewled, pushing back against his finger.  "More," she commanded.

He inserted another finger while she slipped her hand between her legs.  As he plowed her tight channel with his fingers, she toyed with her clit.

"Yeah, sweetheart," he said, leaning over her and gripping her shoulder.  "Are you going to make yourself come while I fuck you?"

"Yes," she cried.

"Good little kitten.  Fuck, I can't wait anymore." Removing his hand, he aligned the tip of his cock with her dewy entrance.  Laura lifted her hips, opening to him as she stimulated her engorged nub.  He jutted inside once...twice...until he was fully sheathed in her body. Then, he began to move, dragging his shaft through her swollen tissues, groaning as he slid back and forth.

"It's heaven, honey," he said, breathing labored as he moved within her. "You're choking me...oh, *god*."

The first hint of climax began to tingle in her spine and she closed her eyes, burying her face in the cushion as he claimed her. His bare skin was steel and softness inside her, all rolled into one. Laura had never had sex without a condom and found the act so intimate.

Adam's palms surrounded her thighs and he leaned over her, the sweaty skin of his chest bracketing her back. "Wrap your legs around me," he growled in her ear.

She complied, encircling his waist with her legs and crossing her ankles behind his back. It was a new angle for her and would've been awkward if he hadn't been there supporting her, holding her stable as he leaned over her. It opened her body in new ways she'd never fathomed and the head of his cock pummeled a spot so sensitive, her toes curled as her eyes rolled back in her head.

"Fuck, kitten," he said in her ear, his voice ragged. "I'm so deep. Take all of me, honey."

"I am," she groaned, throwing her head back to rest on his shoulder. "Oh, Adam...it's never been like this. You feel amazing."

"You were made for me, baby," he said into the shell of her ear. "Made to take my cock. Whose pussy is this?"

"Yours."

"Fuck yes. I love you, Laura. Open up and feel me, honey. I love you so much."

The words shattered her soul, leading to an explosion in her body as she fell over the edge. Her strong man held her, impaling her with his firm hips, clutching her almost desperately. It was moving and passionate, and she screamed his name as he whispered words of desire in her ear. Growling her name, his arms tightened around her and he began to convulse, spurting his release deep into her body, marking her with his essence.

Overcome with love, and the thought that they could be conceiving another child, she clutched him tight with her legs and searched for a stronghold. His hands slid over hers, entwining their fingers as he depleted himself into her tight channel. It was so intimate...so raw...that she felt ripped apart and tears burned her eyes.

"Sweetheart," he whispered, holding her close as his body trembled. A lone tear escaped the corner of her eye and his lips sipped it from her skin. "Please don't cry. Are you okay? Did I hurt you?"

"No," she said, feeling like an idiot as she shook in his arms. "I just never thought I'd find you, Adam. I love you so much. I'd die if I lost you."

"I'm right here, Laura," he said, kissing her temple. "Forever. You're mine."

"I'm yours," she said, snuggling into him.

There, on the couch, they recovered from their lovemaking, not realizing until weeks later they'd conceived a sibling for their beloved Chloe.

# *Epilogue*

♥

***July Fourth, Independence Day, many months later...***

Laura stood with Kayla and Joy, rubbing her distended abdomen as the three of them watched Carter and Sam play with the kids.

"I think Carter needs some lessons on how to color between the lines," Laura said. "He's terrible with the sidewalk chalk. Sam's a natural though."

"Sam's great at everything," Joy said wistfully.

"Carter has a limited skill set but when he's good at something, he's really good." Kayla waggled her eyebrows.

Laughing, Laura slid an arm over each of their shoulders, drawing them close. "Remember all those years ago, when Kayla told us she was entering into a fake relationship with Carter? We were all single and so unlucky in love. Then, it all started to change. We knew her heart didn't stand a chance with him. She was down for the count."

"Don't forget when Joy fell for Sam," Kayla said, grinning. "She kept telling us about the super sweet IT guy. I think she was secretly in love with him for years."

"I probably was," Joy said, gazing at Sam. "He's perfect."

"And then there's you," Kayla said, winking at Laura. "You had to be the difficult one but you got there eventually."

"It's not fun if it's easy guys," Laura said, squeezing them. "And Adam was so worth the wait. Man, I had no idea I could love this deeply. It's something else. Oh, and his massive package doesn't hurt either."

Joy snickered. "Definitely not."

As if she'd conjured him with her words, Adam stepped onto the rooftop dressed in his pristine white naval uniform. He'd attended a morning ceremony in the Bronx with some of the reserve trainees, requiring him to wear the attire. Laura thought him sexy-as-hell and couldn't wait to have him bang her mindless while still in uniform later. How sinfully exciting.

"Pregnant women aren't supposed to lust after men like that, Laura," Kayla teased.

"Can't help it," she murmured. "Holy hotness, guys. Have you ever seen anything as scrumptious? I can't wait to disarm him tonight if you know what I mean."

"Oh, we know, sweetie," Joy said.

"Hey, sweetheart," Adam said as he approached, kissing Laura and then placing a friendly peck on Kayla and Joy's cheeks. "Did you guys take care of my woman while I was gone?"

Laura gave a *pfft* and waved her hand. "Your woman can take care of herself, thank you very much."

"Don't I know it," he said, pulling her into a dramatic embrace. "Excuse me, ladies. I need to kiss my wife properly."

"We'll be over there," Kayla said, tugging Joy's hand so they could join their husbands and kids while Adam parted her lips with his and gave her a stunning kiss. Tingling from head to toe, she gulped in air as she stared up at him once he'd broken the kiss.

"What's gotten into you, soldier?" she asked seductively.

"I just thought about you all day. I mean, it is kind of our anniversary. I met you at a July fourth wedding and found you four years later on that same holiday. It's pretty serendipitous."

"Of course, my sexy soldier would find a way to romanticize Independence Day."

"It will always be special to me, even more so now because of you, honey."

"My patriotic prince," she murmured, caressing the short hair at the back of his neck. "I love you so much."

"I love you too, kitten."

"Daddy," Chloe called, running toward him, clutching his shoulders after he lifted her in his arms. "Did you have fun at work?"

"Not as much fun as we're going to have now. I'm off for three days and we're going to go to the playground and McDonalds and all the museums you want."

"Mommy says we should go to the natural museum. It has dinosaurs."

"That's the Museum of Natural History, baby," Laura said, smoothing Chloe's hair out of her eyes. "And, yes, I think it will be so fun."

"I love you, Mommy," she said, resting her head on Adam's chest. "And I love Daddy too," she whispered, adorable as she bit her lip.

"I love you and Daddy too," Laura said, encircling them with her arms and leaning her cheek against Adam's shoulder.

Locked in the gentle embrace, the family that began from a chance encounter under the stars on a warm beachside evening reveled in the love that made them whole.

Together on the rooftop, the now-complete friend family, comprised of their beloved partners and children, held one of many Independence Day cookouts they would share. Fulfilled and undivided, Laura, Joy, and Kayla celebrated the wondrous notion that they would always be connected and would share their future with every person they loved deep in their souls.

**Happy Independence Day to the soldiers and veterans who keep us safe.  Your sacrifice and service are so appreciated and this author thanks you from the bottom of her heart.**

# Before You Go

Thank you all so much for reading the Manhattan Holiday Loves series. I hope you loved this "friend family" as much as I did! Ready to start a new series with me? I decided to write a steamy, small-town romance series based in the fictional town of Ardor Creek. Check out Book 1, **Hearts Reclaimed**, now! Grumpy widower Scott isn't interested in love but he can't stop thinking about feisty food truck owner Ashlyn.

*Please consider leaving a review on your retailer's site, BookBub and/or Goodreads. Your reviews help spread the word for indie authors so we can keep writing smokin' hot books for you to devour. Thanks so much for reading!*

# Acknowledgments

♥

Thanks to everyone who read and supported this series. It was a fun side project that I never planned on writing, but Kayla, Joy, and Laura appeared in my head, along with their sexy love interests, and I figured, why not? The stories about these funny, flawed, extremely loyal characters made me smile, and if they bring one other person joy in this hectic, stressful world, then it was worth it! Thank you for taking the journey with me!

# About the Author

Ayla Asher is the pen name for a USA Today bestselling author who writes steamy fantasy romance under a different pseudonym. However, she loves a spicy, fast-paced contemporary romance too! Therefore, she's decided to share some of her contemporary stories, hoping to spread a little joy one HEA at a time. She would love to connect with you on social media, where she enjoys making dorky TikToks, FB/IG posts and steamy book trailers!

# ALSO BY AYLA ASHER

**<u>Manhattan Holiday Loves Trilogy</u>**
Book 1: His Holiday Pact
Book 2: Her Valentine Surprise
Book 3: Her Patriotic Prince

**<u>Ardor Creek Series</u>**
Book 1: Hearts Reclaimed
Book 2: Illusions Unveiled
Book 3: Desires Uncovered
Book 4: Resolutions Embraced
Book 5: Passions Fulfilled
Book 6: Futures Entwined